just sitting around
here GRUESOMELY now

THE
SEAGULL
LIBRARY OF
GERMAN
LITERATURE

*just sitting around
here GRUESOMELY now*

FRIEDERIKE MAYRÖCKER

TRANSLATED BY ROSLYN THEOBALD

LONDON NEW YORK CALCUTTA

This publication was supported by a grant
from the Goethe-Institut, India.

Seagull Books, 2022

First published in English by Seagull Books, 2021

English translation © Roslyn Theobald, 2021

ISBN 978 1 8030 9 213 3

British Library Cataloguing-in-Publication Data
A catalogue record for this book is available from the British Library.

Typeset by Seagull Books, Calcutta, India
Printed and bound by WordsWorth India, New Delhi, India

just sitting around
here GRUESOMELY now

haven't moved an inch I'm just sitting around here gruesomely now, I tell Ely, the beginning doesn't seem to be sad enough, Petrarca, the title of my next book perhaps *études*, the plumage unfathomable, there are night moths that drink human tears, I tell Ely, lamenting / lumbering the soul, I say, a mountain's jagged crown a tulip's jagged crown—my doctor called and told me he had slit open his own throbbing finger (the way borderline patients might do).

I was frightened by the rumbling of a storm during the night, I tell Ely, I was horribly frightened, I say, my heart was trembling, I stole over to the door of my flat and peered through the peephole or JUDAS, to see if someone might be there in the corridor approaching my door, but before the JUDAS has faded away, etc., morning comes and I expel a mouthful of saliva onto the floor, I say, where the gladiolas come up, saliva encourages 'gladiolas to come into bloom there'll be an entire forest of gladiolas here, orange-coloured gladiolas lavender-coloured blue, wilted flowers were left at the exit for weeks, gladiolas, stems of lilac, palm leaves, bleeding peonies, *plagiarized*, driving me into a raging mania, *touched by grace*, as per Jean Genet, columbine is also known as the Glove of Our Holy Mother,

MIGNON, I think I've gotten a little confused about how to get on with my writing, I say to Ely, I've grown a little somnambulist, I get an idea, and even when my intellect is not completely unengaged, imagined letters to Rumi or E.S. and writing letters in bed I just keep right on writing off over the edge of the paper onto my featherbed and now my covers are full of little black spots from my marker ...... our bed is our office, I say, a bed is a place for sleeping a bed is a place for writing, sometimes we visit the Botanical Garden (along with our Rose of Adonis), we sat on the podium in the lecture hall and I drew you a bird with wide-open and outstretched wings which means that we will be taking a trip on an aeroplane, I say, individual sentences lined up into suites, complete, the way Couperin worked his Cembalo Concertos, I wake up with the words *'villages nouveau riches'*—

all of a sudden after weeks of extreme heat at some time around 15 past 4 woke up to portents of an oncoming storm, it was as if a giant boulder had broken loose and come thundering down into the valley. The papers on my writing desk flew up into air and swirled around my room and I felt as though my insides were being knotted up into a ball of furious snakes and I had to throw up, all of this taking place over the course of kind dreams, and then the storm fell asleep and the morning breezes settled down into 1 corner of my room, *the entire JOSEPHSTADT dunked deep into a glass full of Henkel*, the 1st birdsong of the morning my summer clothes fragrant bouquets of flowers in the window, all these unlaughing creatures deep in contemplation something shuddered inside me, Brigitte

St telephoned her ill-fated life to me but the fine arts, the moon buried itself in the curtains sleep no longer possible, lamb against the backdrop of a blue heaven is something you often find in Romanesque churches, I read in J.D.'s GLASS, 1 éclat is 1 glittering splinter, my bed cover is beginning to feel damp, I say, when I was a child I remember there was a boy named JOSCHI who always wore a pair of striped bathing trunks and I never wanted to say his name out loud, really I was ashamed to say his name out loud (apparently, according to Jean Genet, he's actually wearing a pair of protective underwear).

As the clematis once did those many summers in D. the bindweed is winding its way up through the *weathered* wooden fence blackened by decades of *weather*. The more hulls there are enclosing a kernel the sweeter it is. Ely and I in the fruit orchard of a local restaurant yesterday, evening, and he said, you're going to write another book of poetry, and I said, it's a dangerous thing, simply beginning to write a new book is a dangerous thing to do—

this forest full of butterflies the forest gnarled full of butterflies, dragonflies doubles of jasmine and I plunged right into it, this forest was full of ancient trees whose trunks were wrapped with rings of iron and whose roots were thick and heavy, feet of tree roots, tables of tree roots, I stumbled along with a heavy heart, reaching for my crew ropes, paced back and forth (was wearing my helmet), dreamt of Ely this night and he kissed me on the forehead and I said I've been worrying about you, I'm worried about you, and he grew petulant, I got lost and it was difficult for me to keep going, I started looking for a clearing and finally found one with gurgling water and there was also a little dog waiting there to lick me, I sat there with Ely and was astounded at what was happening to my own body, how it was failing me drying up on me, stunned at what was hurting and crippled, etc., the way I kept losing my footing as if I were traversing an ice-covered field light was dripping from the thick leafy canopies overhead I believe it brought the ltl. deer out of hiding, we struggled to make our way to Vlado's housing complex and he was already up standing on his balcony and waving a welcome to us!, Wertheimsteinpark. In my slumber growing awareness of the sounds of my own breathing and I am surprised and I feel guilty or ashamed.

Damp crowns on my forehead brush, these bushy eye-lashes, 1st of March evening : the hour of budding, I am made up of primitive reflexes, I say, the language I am thinking of, I say, delicate and fragile : my spirit my character (Ely objected to the word character)—

the word *throw* (found in Ponge's 'Pine Forests') reminds me of a scene, I say, where Musette or Mama covered the divan the couch the sofa with a threadbare *throw* that had once been used to cover a car, i.e. she spread the threadbare blanket over my bed forming precisely 1 set of *cascading folds*. I am ill, I am dehydrated, I have a cramp in my leg, I see things, sinking into emptiness without the slightest idea of what is going on, or it was an albatross and I'd dug my claws into the feathers of an albatross, I say, my tears like drops of perspiration on my face, our host's garden flickering full of flying bushes and trees and we dove in, budding clouds and realms of gushing waters, we sat across from each other and I saw how his eyes studied the sorrows of this landscape, his eyes searched everywhere in every direction and so my tears. He seemed to be moved by the depth of the beauty in this garden with its winding paths steps and niches, magical arches made of fig trees and grapevines and perfect silence, the birds were silent, on the branches over our heads—he had begun *to weave* my pale fingers again as they lay flat on the garden table, we were both enchanted by this play, *a photographer's panicle*, thimble lilies forget-me-nots, the wilted rose leaf stuck to the edge of a drinking glass—the squalls were dreadful frightening and I wake up to a tiger's eye the size of a postage stamp watching me pleading for an outing to the zoo at Schönbrunn, etc., exchange of letters exchange of glances, the yng. stranger at KONSUM greeted me with a smile and lay his hand across his heart, 'and without missing a beat fluttering' (Nina Jäckle)

through the peephole / the espionage hole / JUDAS I see Musette or my mother sitting all hunched up, she has just had all of her incisors pulled, and I was wearing a brightly coloured silk blouse with long sleeves to hide my thin arms, I could smell my own body's sweat, dream interrupted, dark slimy discharge from my left (sick) eye, a morning's silence complete this *apricot-coloured* sky in my window frame, inhale deeply this morning's *apricot-coloured* freshness but no birdsong, my hydrangea soul, drag myself to the large wide-open window ('landscape'), peeling apart of my dreams. I remember, I used to always skip dessert intending to be thin, was about 17 .. ('the ltl. Genet is doing the same thing'), we were sitting above a gully in the full midday heat and Ely said 'this stench', it was the hospital quarter, the doctors were running around in their white coats, a chaos of running around in white ROBES, etc. 1 small tooth, all this noise for 1 small tooth 1 very delicate and sweet sound I was having breakfast at my little drop-leaf table in the kitchen what was I eating an exquisitely sweet distant sound of bells ringing like 1 small tooth what was it, back and forth, I ran all over the neighbourhood, it was 1 small tooth, 1 ltl. hook on the wall 1 small tooth had worked its way loose 1 small hook on the wall had worked its way loose, *I mean the buttercups* of course these meadows covered in thousands of butter-cups, provoking provocative redolent with the taste of fresh butter on my tongue, isn't that so, 'into the grave having consumed tons of food' .. (Genet), these butter-cups in the forest imparting a brilliance to the bread in the breadbox still steaming warm, this ltl. letter slid to the upper corner of the bed this sml. letter in print, folded into a ltl. letter this paper at the exit, Ponge writes about 'momenting', perhaps I have a 'religious nature', as Ponge has written : *which has simply crushed everything inside me and around me—*

here at my window on this morning everything smells like the ADRIATIC (Jesolo, Cattolica), *actually I've just been sawed through by universum*, sashes of light, my night is still holding its breath, the angel's trumpet tree, my doctor says, is ripping your pupils open, the wisteria trembling in your hand, my pupils ripped open, having feelings in my eyes I've been shattered. In the hallway closet run across that pair of white woollen gloves they'd been folded into each other, are glowing in my direction : 1 dusty washed-out white, I say, next to my umbrella sleeve, as for these shocking glacé gloves, I say to Ely, I had a pair of them at 1 time, but later, only 1 single 1 still in my possession, exquisite sword- lance gladiola, 'I go back into the kitchen and find my gloves there and the *odour of my teeth* as well', according to Jean Genet, columbine = the Glove of Our Holy Mother, etc.

Both plane trees, as seen from the balcony, had grown into the tendrils of a lime tree which now hung down to the ground, blossoms in labour, from the canopy of the tree the limbs plunging downwards stroking the ground, it rained stormed and raged all night through while bolts of lightning flashed through my closed eyelids like the lights on a Christmas tree, Ely and I ate from sticky plates, the ltl. slope only to be navigated with the assistance of a collection of men's umbrellas bundled together for the purpose, I say.

The way E.S. *straightens* my jacket for me, I tell Ely, fits it to me actually elongating it, I say to Ely, I am pulling this text together, I mean setting it right, setting this text right, I say ('O eternity, you word thunder'), end of February, the 2nd budding hike is about to take place, I say

Heat so extreme, I say, that any blouse I put on was wet through within a few minutes, any blouse I take off was dry within a few minutes, and me being hounded down one of these narrow streets because of my knee, because it felt to me as though my left knee were broken—and because I was no longer able to tolerate my reflection in the mirror and because the angel's trumpets were blowing so wildly in the wind their hly. leaves swaying wildly from side to side, I mean the powerful winds of this storm tore the windows out of their housings and they crashed to the ground and shattered, and this is what happened to us during the grt. storms, we were shaken to the core to our centres, etc. We buy pink file folders, I mean the *claws of the emergency binder*, according to Ely, sunspots on cloth aprons silverfish on floor tiles, 40 years ago I remember, Ely said, please visit me soon, the dawning light of day will crown your head, I will run out to meet you in the hallway when you ring at the door to my building—

now manic myself, according to Ely, when you say, *I am your ivy*, I'll go down on my knee I see myself going down on my knee when you say I am your ivy, according to Ely, 'my pleasant trans-alpine loneliness, the beginning still doesn't seem sad enough', Petrarca, the lrg. pair of scissors in this case for my glasses, on Sunday afternoon looking forward to Monday, I say, fresh beginning to the week, etc.

1 utter Shame 1 utter Fall 1 utter Notre Dame, I say, the petals of the columbine, the *dancings* ...... Max Ernst planted columbines because it is a flower of melancholy, after daytime sleep not knowing whether morning or

night truly disoriented, 1 subtle twist 1 subtle gesture, before we actually meet each other again discover each other again, isn't that so, where have you been, I ask Ely, I've been in a kind of half sleep, or was I only a fiction, in my mind's eye someone with a hedge clipper and pruning shears raging through the garden in D., forging right through the lush green garden in D., cutting down all the flowers gathering all the flowers, apparently Musette or Mama, I say to Ely, in her dress and fur apron, roaming around the garden, cutting something here *snipping away* at a few things there, here and there, lilies asters wisteria iris, I see her, Musette or Mama wandering through the garden in D. with a hedge clipper / lrg. pair of pruning shears as *table ornamentation* for the lrg. green wooden table on the patio, and still everything so uncertain

('The Emotions of Flowers', J.D.) 1 part decorative flowers 1 part decorative labyrinth, kitchen herbs growing up the posts of the fencing, in the strawberry beds the slugs, I say, the genre and subject of this picture merely suggested. As far as the garden in D. is concerned, I say to Ely, either Musette or Mama is on the way there with a sickle and the moon to *harvest* mallow white lilies wisteria and iris to make 1 single bouquet of bundled pieces of cuckoo I mean ...... in order to *fit out* this endeavour with bird feathers I mean ...... I mean RUMI had the swallows darting through the air ('btt!, btt!, btt!), this morning the brushwood in the flower pot, I say to RUMI, have climbed 2 globes myself, one of the old world and one of the new, I say, what happened then, I say to RUMI, would you really have been able to imagine it even in your wildest dreams, I

climbed up onto 2 globes and opened my arms, that is
after all the life of a poet, I say, I strolled through gardens
of gorse and opened my arms wide, I can't really tolerate
people around me *just mouthing off*, I strolled through the
streets of Venice the perfect ruins as perfect as I imagine
ruins to be, the palazzi under water. I wanted to travel
there with RUMI but I lost the courage to do it and I sent
him encoded dispatches instead ...... the *colossal* features
of my face in the hallway mirror when I dart around any
number of times at night on my way to my own crucifixion
or resignation, I say, this oozing soul in the estrly. window,
I say to RUMI, I cannot bear this unbearable Glory or
gloire, it was an abstract love, it was an utterly mad plan
stark raving mad, I say to RUMI, the unforgiving light from
the skylight, and no one had an awning to offer me, o, I
said to RUMI, you simply gave no thought to who might be
ready to provide you with an awning, and there was 1
night when I lost the very marrow in my bones, I say, I
remember, Christa K. said, he gave me a rose-patterned
awning for my terrace, so that I could look out at the lake
without *straining* my eyes, the sun was glistening glimmering off the surface of a lake full of 'waves of silver'
(Höld.)

this is my beloved Traun on whose banks I have often lain
dreaming and deep in thought, I tell Dufy, she goes into
the lake and makes her way around it and leaves somewhat warmed by its waters. this is my beloved High
Traun, these mysterious thrashing waters source in the
mountains rise frothing into a veritable swan heaven, etc.

While he, Ely, puts his tennis shoes back on so as not to have to make his way back in while exposing his pure white socks to the dust encrusted I mean the *dust parlour*, where my *flowers eyes* on the floor, he said, Ely, 'Dufy the Danube' is a delightful river : if you ever get in you'll never get out alive, Brigitte Schwaiger—

1 Soaking Wet Sweatshirt, according to Ely.

We're going to leave tomorrow, I tell Dufy, you will open the curtains and take a look at the lake, I mean you will take a look at the Traunsee with its swans, a look at the mountain range to the south. Me wearing an elderberry-coloured jacket in a riot of blossoms my reflection in the mirror, I say, as if the surrounding forest were somehow a picture of me, my image, a reflection me, the way I am being informed infused with the bowed ancientness of this *region* such wondrous beauty in 1 word that simply came to me in the interiors of this forest, labyrinth at the forest's edge—here I stand at the edge of the forest and stare into its glimmering eye its sunset I mean thus seduced. As to the opening of arms, I say, as to open arms, I ran up to Emmy W. with open arms, I recognized her from a distance, I say, my (with open arms) relationship to language, etc. During an extended journey by car holding the distant mountains close to my heart, I say, and in the background the snow-covered mountains : no, said Ely, a range of white mountainous clouds, Gmunden am See, the point at which wild white mountain ranges displaced each ground into 1 another over 1 another, under 1 another, they crawled these forested blue-grey blue-green like sapphires while the spirits of the lake, I say, iris,

gladiolas, I mean the *sickle and moon* forging on through
the glimmering garden in D., and song of songs like, I say
to Ely, and as far as the lrg. black hare is concerned, in the
field surrounding the farmhouse in Rohrmoos, I understand he can barely hop any longer—all we hear from that
quarter is zither music. An erotic dream, Ely kissed me on
the palm of my left hand actually on my RING FINGER, he
has been keeping his hairbrush in the hallway closet for
11 years, Emmy W. in my direction with open arms in
the hotel breakfast room : scattering bushels of meadow
blossoms over our table, etc.

Having to listen to Mozart makes me throw up, the feeling
of ecstasy we get from a scent makes us drunk, isn't that
so, I say to Ely, this sense we have for scent throws us off
balance the expectation of sensing 1 very specific scent
captures us and our entire body of senses is awakened, it's
been a very long time since we've had such a mysteriously
ambivalent experience, etc., autumn has opened its eye,
says E.S., and as far as the Baths at CAMAIORE are concerned, I say to Ely, Dufy has been standing at the window
of this hotel room for a long time, already opened the curtains and is enjoying the view of the sea and the beaches of
CAMAIORE—then he put his hands to his temples focused
on this part of the sea and the coastline, and it seemed to
me as if I had become him : I had transformed myself into
him and been infused with the mystery and the joy of this
view of the open sea and the shoreline at CAMAIORE, the
rising moon in a sky-blue heaven, we were wandering along
the promenade, I say to Ely and I sense the beginning of
the end of summer, I said, while the seagulls I mean this

soaring of heads over the course of the tricolour of the evening. 1 utterly excessive scene as Dufy opens the curtains, puts his hands to his temples and that's the way he imagines this scene himself, the way this scene enthrals him, just the way he would paint this scene himself. Full sails full sails ahead, out onto the tricolour of the sea, the glimmering dusk, the horizon, I mean I remember Daphne's appearance : a Daphnesque brush with rose-coloured calyx, with rose-coloured crown (Sonatas), *a gallant Wind*, Ely remarked, *an allegro intellect* : 1 time *here* 1 time *there*, the scratchiest of worlds, etc.

I crossed myself, but with sickle and moon still forging on through the glimmering garden 'where 2 souls glow into each other', Adalbert Stifter.

The lake was glittering without having been touched by 1 single ray of sunlight and 1 single swan was visible gliding across its surface, enchanted moon enchanted sun at ½ past 3 in the morning she woke up to the white blonde figure of Indian Summer embracing her the mountains sank into the lake and in the late evening it grew cooler and she started to shiver, they took a walk along the promenade wandering around until they began to get tired and the TRAUNSTEIN enveloped itself in red, the fact that the TRAUN flows into the TRAUNSTEIN, as is widely known, and flows out of the Traunsee at a specific location astounded her, and she asked Ely if there were a way to find the Traun again once it had exited the Traunsee— wondering if the Traun might assume a distinctive colour or a special flow, wondering if there might be a way to recognize the Traun again, etc., she seems to have fallen in love with the river.

This oozing and dripping was a handicap on my part, and as we spent the afternoons on our hot balcony : lying in our rocking chairs or hunched up in our rattan beach chairs our eyes on the wildest of bushes, leaves floating by, twinning branches of a low-hanging lime tree, the echoes of heavenly trumpets going lost somewhere inside my heart, I mean the torrent of thick leafy crowns of this impenetrable foliage fluttering down from the trees leaves seeping down through the trees, etc., while the *immense* leaves of our fig tree at the entrance to the garden continue to stroke our foreheads and flutter into our eyes, and me, once we are inside this garden, especially me, the damp stone steps and air roots of the exotic tree giants which I with open arms, and I say to Ely, 'these dreams come out of nowhere and disappear back into nowhere again,' my dream of a figure *overflowing* which in the meantime, over the course of a few hours, had already resolved.

she had been ensnared in a forest catastrophe of purple spring, had been *on her way* to a cemetery in the forest : I mean the heavily veiled elderly woman I saw on the train, she was *on her way* to a funeral in the Provinces *on her way* to a funeral in a forest cemetery, I say to Ely, it was my doctor *on her way* to her husband's funeral in the forest— a fact she never shared outright or at least never made clear she merely hinted at happenings and almost in whispers as I recall I remember that brief conversation I had with her on her mobile phone and my intuition told me more than the facts she imparted, and after all these years I recall this incident, I say to Ely, everything I recall is vague and uncertain it's a portrait done in the clouded light of my fantasy and not a reality (like the kisses of a forest full of laurel that seemed to be coming my way), she is ensnared in a forest catastrophe of purple spring, in my eyes, I say to Ely, she was in a compartment on the train with her hands in her lap holding a funereal bouquet etc., *on her way*

Claw in notebook, gecko in the wash basin, we were in love, we were very much in love *with white shirts*, on the train no seats free on the train so we crouched in the corridor near the WC and we sank into 1 another sank into 1 another, in the car I folded my hands and said, *I have these coloraturas*, etc.

And this orange-coloured notebook, according to Ely, you should record all the passages and memories you have of me in your notebook, and when you're about to break down in tears, Ely says, and when the orange-coloured and rose-coloured binders we've bought for these notebooks, if this actually is a sign I mean, if this actually is a sign of an orange-coloured and rose-coloured spring, 1 in which the blossoms of a new spring aren't yet in bud, haven't yet set any buds—these glowing orange-coloured and rose-coloured folders for the notebooks I want you to use for everything you have to say to me, record all the passages and memories you have of me, memories of the love we both have for Mimmo Paladino and Sandro Chia, I mean this WORK ON PAPER like Mimmo Paladino's, e.g. the ones with numerous drafts of 'Man with Dog on a Park Bench with Spring in Bud', I mean the very last moments before awakening before waking up in the morning, these are the silver threads of my morning, the silver threads which lead me into my day and give me my words and my plans which do not or do come to fruition in 1 form or another, the way/ways in which you imagine a black silk jacket or a Molino cardigan in the morning a very few seconds before the glow of a new day, I mean the silver threads which lead you into your day, according to Ely, no, I say, not *these beggarly little dots*, I'm looking for a well-worked ending to a sentence, I don't mean these mad = beggarly little dots at the end of a sentence, or (even) at the end of a book, as in the past, there was the appearance of midday on the wooden benches under the lush leafy canopies of Bad Ischl, us at a midday table, a midday meal, crowns of maple trees swayed in spring breezes and feathers of birds (of memory), claws of binders, etc., sweetly slanting slope or honey, I mean.

The Pulkau, this agile little stream, had grown into a mighty river, I say to Ely, Zellerndorf, Hadres, Pulkau were flooded, in gardens rose bushes bleeding faded flattened, I mean downright *bandaged*, walking on crutches.

A *flooded* figure appeared to me in my dreams but melted away the way clouds melt into the sky, a few hours passed and I dreamt of Picasso's Harlequin or Clown with Metal

Framed Glasses, of his 'pink period', once a table became free we moved into the shade, and Ely said, 'the movie screen in front of us, the TV crate,' I mean a group of art students sitting across the table in quiet conversation and 1 of the young women with perfect hair, etc., (Nam June Paik on the air as 'TV Buddha') *was crouching there on her heels*, a gracious breeze, Ely said

it's the truth it's a clap of thunder, the sparks had leapt away. And we were *frozen furtively*, fled into a sml. inn whose window had begun to *glow* as we approached it : be it a reflection from the evening sun or be it *heat* (us pleading) from the oven on the inside, we, Ely and I went into the bar and soon our cheeks began to glow

the sweet red blossoms of the oleander in front of the Opera House that remind one of small red roses, the kind Muzette or Mama are so fond of I kissed stood ankle-deep in the garden over air roots of giant trees, etc., *I salivated*, Ely said, 'once I would like to take the Trans-Siberian Railway several days and nights,' I mean like the trip we took to Moscow and St Petersburg in 1978 when I lay DELIRIOUSLY in the Sleeping Car the night after the raging light of the Neva, something like Neva Nerves, the steaming bassin = public swimming pool in the middle of the city this frigid spring, the sky over the Neva bright as day there were tones of pure light without any night chirping I mean the waves of the Neva broke against the landing and I was afraid I was going to plunge into the waters, you see, I told Ely, do you remember once when I was reading Kleist's novella 'The Marquise of O.' a friend called and I found myself responding in a way, I mean I *intentionally* expressed myself in a way I otherwise would not have and thus surprising even myself hurriedly returned to Kleist's novella. Even though in my own country I thought myself in Italy, I say to Ely, it was a happily wondrous illusion, do you remember, I say to Ely, even though in our own country we thought ourselves in Italy's mountain meadows and lakes I mean something like the shores of Lake Como, even at the Adriatic, and only because in the company of an Italian friend Luigi R., because we with him the shores of Lake Traun and the Tricolours, I say to Ely, how could Lake Traun suddenly transpose itself into Italian waters simply through the presence of an Italian friend, I say to Ely, what do you think, I say, we strolled along the shoreline promenade of Lake Traun and thought ourselves in Italy under Italian skies and in Italian gardens where lemons on every pale bush—the way it was back then in the gardens of Hotel Lord Byron in Rome. And so the Salzkammergut transformed itself into Italian mountain meadows and lakes, simply because at our side our Italian friend, you see, I say to Ely, he had been able to WONDROUSLY TRANSPOSE our own mountains and lakes onto Italian mountains and lakes I mean through his simple presence, you see, we took him by the hand and wandered along the shores of our own lake, while actually thinking ourselves on Italian shores / seashores, how had that come about. As the hour of his departure drew near, you see, goodbyes were difficult, goodbyes were difficult for both parties and for quite some time we took consolation in our friend's eyes *while the bitter orange* how can we possibly know, as Elke Erb said, how a sweet ltl. bird feels when it *chirps itself away* into the spheres of Dante's Paradise, with rejoicing song a brilliant beacon, etc. Sitting like a tailor in the middle of a carpet in her flat I see her speaking to me and she is telling me that to her my words are gloriose and they have simply shaken her *to the very marrow*—and when all of a sudden I squeezed an entire bouquet of flowers, I say to Ely, gillyflowers, anemones tree ferns and Fr. hibiscus the only real thing that blooms up in me is the name of these flowers but not their appearance and so I am deceiving her, *these blossom crowns* and so I feign knowledge of botany while simply scribbling down a few flower names, I mean the 1's that simply come to mind simply fall like rain 1 rainfall—still half asleep she is sealing her lips with a strand of hair.

The raging storms overnight, I say to Ely, and second by second those flashes of lightning following 1 another, and I still lying in bed my eyelids tightly closed, I, produced in me the sensation of 1 of those New Year's Eves when I was frightened that the fireworks exploding all around us would surely come crashing down on the flat roof of our building explode and set it on fire—

1 small pen 1 limp sheet of paper some time around the middle of August 1 small pen in my dessous, I say to Ely, leaves of coltsfoot, 1 enlarged photograph of Tischbein's *Portrait of Johann Wolfgang von Goethe* on the wall, 'seeing the bottle *as such* is seeing the bottle the way it would be without me,' J.D. says, 'if I were dead the bottle would simply retain the same character it has now it would have the same colour the same consistency and so forth.' When I'm at St Stephen's Square and stand there looking up at

St Stephen's Cathedral I know that St Stephen's Cathedral would still be standing there if I were dead : it would be standing there exactly as it is standing there now and life would simply go on the way it goes on now. When the afternoon sun catches fountain waters gushing, rising waters falling waters of the central fountain at 1 certain angle in all its pastel shades, it might happen, a rainbow so compelling and of such beauty might begin to arc over the Square that our eyes, beguiled and blinded both, will have to turn away, don't you see, I say to Ely

how they rained down. When started looking for 1 of my books on my bookshelf to give it to a friend, I say to Ely, *oh how they rained down*. *A crooked pony* in a picture that is 10 years now, I say, you had it framed and now I've got it on the little table I use for my typewriter, your whip is out, we're listening to Billie Holiday and John Dowland, cleaned the case for my glasses with a hand vacuum. Your new style, Ely says, appearing to be repetitive narration, is compelling, Ely says, *a kind of incantation*. Because my spine is crooked, I say, I often have difficulty swallowing and minor episodes of choking—and then I saw the pit of a plum on the kitchen floor and 1 strand of black wavy hair on my white tablecloth

all night long kept making notes *in fits and starts* so hardly slept at all and in the morning when I wanted to make a clean copy had no mental strength to do it : kisses full of laurels WERE NOT TO BE, so exhausted ('on peaks most separate', Höld.)

(P.S. *plucked gesture* of a yng. swan on Lake Traun, placing 1 leg across his back IN ORDER TO REST, *plucked gesture* of a yng. waitress placing 1 arm across her back in order to express her competence to serve, her readiness to take orders from her customers, etc., what she actually wants to say, you see, is that despite all this competence she is not in the least willing to get anywhere near her customers). I have an old faded photograph, I say to Ely, in which my young parents are pictured in a Bowling Club obviously dedicated to the sport, but I am not in the picture not in this photograph at all, my father is beginning his approach to the lane and he rolls the heavy ball towards two rows of pins set up at the other end of the alley—I am absent from this picture. Absent from our cafe is the exceptionally polite elderly gentleman who every time he sees me half stands up (a not entirely accomplished bow) and smiles at me a shower of blossoms I meet him in the pharmacy where I go almost every day and ask him if he lives in our neighbourhood and he answers with a smile explaining that he has no home anywhere, his face is pale his face is spiritual a glow in his eyes which I find enthralling.

I have forgotten Goethe's 1st name, a stream of tears when I overhear a yng. flood victim speaking broken English, '1 tent 1 cot 1 muddy bicycle and that's all,' he says, *1 shower of blossoms*, I say to Ely, my eyes veiled in tears in half shade, I say to Ely, out of the large window of the restaurant I see the fronds of 2 potted palms swaying in the southerly wind, my agitation—

my agitation my (agile) mountain world my tears my beloved life from which I do not intend to separate myself, etc., things *buttered* the yellow secret of the buttercups or marsh marigold which looked like something dreamt : a rain soaked field : I believe I actually saw it once a something which caused me to tremble, I say to Ely, it once happened in dawn's red glow I found myself having to cry because my soul was being (*stretched open*) by an incomprehensible yearning, I say to Ely, Roberta and Vlado on the balcony while their eyes *into the green* of 2 cypress trees, in the area of the Cobenzl, 'under the heavens' the rondeau of the TREES OF LIFE

I have *mouches volantes*, I say to Ely, this fly in front of my eyes, I say, it is reeling in front of my eyes, the last breath of summer, I say, the pussy cat, themes, I've been writing down themes all night long, observing the swallows the way they flew in and out of the sml. windows of the stall, the rose-coloured umbels the rose-coloured brush in the corridor, the rose-coloured hortensia (clouds) wilted clouds in the corridor, soaked with sweat the sofa cushions smelt of wet leather and made me sick in the morning and now I'm dreaming and now I'm fantasizing, I'm folding my hands, I'm reining in the weekdays slippery as fishy things. Slipping out of consciousness : hardly Monday evening already early Friday morning, etc., stop! stop! stay right where you are!

P.S. ('I mean as far as Raoul Dufy's Beech Trees is concerned as far as maladied painting and writing persons are

concerned, what we're dealing with is excerpts from
the visible and invisible, world, I say to Ely, and so if you
lay hands on both temples, you see, you construct 1
windowscape : 1 miniature room, miniature box, 1
camera obscura as we are familiar with it in the works of
Raoul Dufy, etc., as we strolled through avenues of yng.
plantings *in dawn's red glow* and I asked him, Ely, what
kind of trees?, he said, he assumed yng. hornbeam trees,
which *in dawn's red glow*')

Angelika K., I say, travels from time to time to a sml.
Polish town ZEBRZYDOWICE where she spends the day with
friends, I say, when I ask why, what attracts you to that
place, she ponders and says, it is the name of the city, the
squares and streets almost devoid of human presence, it is
like velvety moss, it is like a forest catastrophe, it is as if
you are entering a golden wheat field, etc., why, what makes
you do it, what takes you to this sml. Polish town once a
month, I say, where you share the streets with local FARM
LABOURERS who still pick their crops by hand, I say. Even
I've had my palm read there and until everything that was
prophesied has come true, I say. In the cemetery of this
sml. town simply paper-flower decoration. And so with
open arms and wings, as I came up to her, I mean in the
breakfast room of our hotel, as I flew in her direction with
wide open arms, although I was uncertain that it actually
was her (she a vision etc.) I *trampled* on my dreams, I left
my concert grand piano to Bodo H., I heard Schubert's
'Trockne Blumen', the dark fruits of the baobab tree trilled
around in my entire body, I prayed a *troubled* Lord's Prayer,
damp fronds of phlox in the gardens in the morning

I am a good person but I am also a hyena, I say to Ely, I am looking for Gerhard Richter's *Landscapes*, I have ordered Jean Genet's *Festival of the Dead*—as far as the potted rhododendrons in the hallway, as far as the potted rose-coloured phlox in the hallway are concerned, I say, their fronds are bowing, they are bowing down to the floor, they are bowing down to the marshy earth I mean they are, they are constantly wilting, this tender (melancholy) state of wilting this flood of tears.

'*She's not like the rest of us,*' that's what the family always said about her when she was mentioned at all, I mean MY MIDDLE WOMAN (*Mitteltante*, like Jean Paul's *Mitteltinte*), she had curly raven-black hair which she kept into old age, she was musical and played the piano well, she was obsessively neat, I believe, *made of hard wood*, she slumped over forward to her death, at the time she, her silk dress painted with poppies, was about to move, you see, she slumped down into a soft red meadow full of poppies, in which she was found, was found by her relatives, that is, covered with poppies, buried under poppies, which she herself was to mow.

Torn apart by cheap imitations. The earth is cooling down *in dawn's red glow. Scraps of Lion* or *Alpine Light* by Man Ray.

The potted hortensia in the corridor have changed colour, I say to Ely, just had a flash or a forest catastrophe, a jack-daw just rushed by and cast a shadow, for 1 brief second, I cut the tip of my finger on the middle finger of my left hand, I lunged at a sml. pile of broken glass on the kitchen floor, I spread my arms wide open made a dive for it, but I was only playing a role, I say to Ely. *A conceited gloire, you see,* all the arrogance of the hops spreading across our window, I say, an aversion to stealing will very likely conceal a profound need to steal something, over the course of a night under a veil of early spring, 1 horse carriage with flickering lamps on each side. 1 collier with bands of rubber around its neck as we stop in front of the jewellery shop to look at their display and Ely asked me ...... but I have never worn jewellery of any sort, the jackdaw sailed past the window, casting a pale shadow across the drapes, from time to time the yng. swans on Lake Traun a leg across their backs in order to rest, *it was a contemplative motif,* as Ely says, it bled through that night—

it is the end of August and I am reaching for the mittens I was wearing last winter my wounded finger like a rotten banana on the table top, I was gripped *in dawn's red glow* 1 sml. box inside which 1finger sheath, the vagrants, the *unspeakable* sick bed, in another sml. box the *unspeakable* love letters between me and Ely, the most wanted posters, the death announcements with funereal borders like the ones Georg Kierdorf-Traut is sending to friends, because so many friends are dying, constantly they are dying inexorably, strays in unfamiliar surroundings, etc., while we in the KONSUM market begin with the yng. woman of a LOWER CLASS I mean with fake diamonds on her upper lip and a yng. pug in her arms a conversation, you see. This *deafening* light of August I say to Ely, here I do nothing else here I am unable to do anything else but tremble, you see, because in an unfamiliar apartment = in the flat of dear and beloved friends (Roberta and Vlado) I am looking for the toilet—and find myself feeling exposed and even endangered, and why? while on the balcony half-screened *by a Spanish wall* the mighty crowns of the forest I mean the bowing heads of the linden trees trail down into the oak gushing forth as if a green waterfall torrent of manes which ......

'The language of flowers'—I stammered, unable to find the words I was looking for, they were sitting in a heap back at the streetcar stop waiting with half-closed eyes for the next tram.

As soon as I wake up, the oppressive image of my troubles, *having to carry* a heavy suitcase up the endless stairs to station exit in Linz and me broken down in tears and no one coming to my assistance (holding 1 hand over the area of his heart, pointing to me, wanting me to know that my feelings and my fate are his, you see, with his other hand grabbing hold of my case causing it to soar to the top of the stairs and then setting it down at my feet he disappears)

and so the sublime glycinias. Scraps of lion, or when I start thinking about it, there's a scrap of flesh from the tip the middle finger of my left hand, maybe I should examine my wound a little more closely with the help of a magnifying glass, I say to Ely, and because I am examining my wound with the help of a magnifying glass, the sight of my wound troubles me in the extreme because I actually do see there is a scrap of flesh *like 1 elderberry*. I am however uncertain whether it is a real wound or a feigned 1 (the way beggars pretend to be lame or blind, etc.)

A collection of sml. bundles of grass, I say to Ely, back then in Rome, I say, these hanging forests of glycinias, I mean, *I am taking care of our need for fresh air*, 1 hike along a meadow lane that leads into the innermost reaches of the forest, I mean the similarity of Gerhard Richter to Caspar David Friederich, I say, or landscapes unfocused. *The Table* by Gerhard with its extended and exaggerated legs and the BECLOUDED ROMANTIC of its top, I mean, as far as this *Table* by Gerhard Richter is concerned, with its wild tabletop, I am touched by its strange and odd look, same family as my ltl. typewriter table with its grim slopes and angles that keep me worrying the whole construct will simply collapse, etc.

P.S. ('As far as my supply of winter boots is concerned, I say to Ely, my *shoe chest* which is spread out all over my flat simply brings me to tears, I mean, e.g. hiding the likes of Jesus Christ under my kitchen chair') my mouth works, I say, and me *howling*, 'I will have to brush my teeth' it is a dizzying view it is a dizzying world, I say to Ely, when I look at his, Gerhard Richter's, paintings I never know how to interpret the happenings, they are in a constant state of fascinating rapture, you see, they can be understood in 1 way or another, I say, and everything seems to be repeated, I say, Vlado keeps coming out onto his balcony to call us in for a visit

the souls I mean the 1's in black coaches that are driven
around the city in covered coaches with black horses and
flickering lanterns on both sides of the carriage, at night,
in the softest nights of spring. But you aren't supposed
to look at them at all : presumably the souls of friends I
once loved

in my latest work, I say to Ely, beauty and rigour will
prevail, I say. As far as the view onto sunfilled branches of
a giant chestnut tree is concerned, I say, on a late August
afternoon, as viewed from the cafe of the city park, it was
as though given a hint of Paradise—and as I was unable to
turn my eyes away, even though everywhere around me
conversations of friends, as daylight faded and the view
which reminded me of the view from the hotel window in
CAMAIORE (Dufy), and this gripped me, full of tears, more
and more and pained me as if it were a leave taking from
this world and a view into another world which even
though of grt. beauty, frightened me, etc.

On the blood-pressure monitor my heart (Jesus) pierced
by an arrow, and a bandage, to stop the bleeding, and so I
had to wonder whether or not it was as indication of heart
disease, a rush = a murmur of my weight (61.3 K), the
fluttering winds of August. 'Hike until you reach the far
side of the forest, on the Danish island MØN, and you will
see the ocean and the rest of the world' : message on a
postcard from MØN Denmark, just put the sharp recently
purchased *paring knife* back in its sheath, you see, in order
to prevent an injury (cut finger, loss of middle finger of
the left hand, etc.)

and so 1 Jesus heart on the monitor, 1 sash across my left
(bare) shoulder, I say, COSTUME or devotions, etc., as if by
accident or by choice and I contemplate my reflection in
the mirror, back then, in D., in the rain barrel filled to the
rim with rainwater, surrounded by *iris* (*iris germanica*)
grown rampant. How could I tell the twins apart, I say to
E.S., were their eyes a different colour : IRIS, rainbow-hued
skin tones, were their ltl. socks of a different colour, did
they have different haircuts or—she answered no, they
have a different look, she says, I have always been able to
tell them apart by their look, likely with high set : *riding*
blades blooms and free vessels, I mean from the very 1st
moment I saw them I could tell them apart by their look,
you see, she said, *it is their inner look*, it is our eyes after
all that open up into our souls 'from a distance I hear
myself saying everything I write / ragingly,' J.D. 1 bloom :
hortensia bloom turning itself in the corridor, having
turned itself around like a sml. faded shrivelled-up skull,
turned in upon itself : like the face of that elderly woman
at the table next to ours in the garden restaurant : a kind
of death's head, consuming itself, shrivelled—I mean the
potted hortensia in the corridor, I say to Ely, by now
completely wilted, turned in upon itself (like 1 self in
contemplation) in the stale water in the blue vase or
among the grass shoots in the garden / inwardly.

Flag is *pavilion*, a soft yelp in the 1st hours of the night,
almost as soft as birdsong, a nursing infant nurses at
everything, E.S. says, looks everywhere for a source of
nutrition, nurses at its mother's cheek and thereby red
maceration, E.S. says, trap sprung, and he often cuts

himself, etc. At Stilitano's feet nothing but leaps of young deer, Jean Genet says. 1 tender seedpod of linden tree on my bed, blown in overnight, I say to Ely, likely soul of a night moth *and I break down in tears*, an amateur sleeper, I say, I lay awake for a number of hours over the course of the night, *by night-time storms immortalized*, etc.

It was an abstract attraction, I say, the poppy seeds on the tablecloth, traces of felt-tip pen on a white baseball cap and today, on the last day of August, I bought a pair of *department-store gloves*, I say to Ely, and the mittens I was wearing last winter finally turned up again, my beret and muff too, etc., I curled in my uninjured index finger in order to protect it, and when I wanted to pick something up instead of reaching with my wounded middle finger, the 1 in need of protection, I reached with my healthy index finger, carefully enough to protect it, I say. I was unable to send the postcards I had bought in Gmunden from Gmunden to friends, for the most part I simply brought them home with me from my trip to Gmunden and I made every effort to send the cards, which pictured various parts (rosettes) of Gmunden, from Vienna to my friends but I was incapable of doing it, it simply did not make any sense to me to send empty postcards (but for a stamped rosette), I could not send greetings from the town I had left some time ago, *despite great ardour*, I say to Ely, the view of Gmunden was abstract, I say, but the abstract view of Gmunden was able to enchant in a way the real one had not done.

I wake up with the words MY CHIEF KARLSPLATZ, wings of linden-tree seedpods spread wide on the white baseball cap, the calluses on the soles of my feet make walking difficult, *I mean rosettes* just sitting around hands folded in the leafy greenery

in my district the sml. death's heads of hortensia, shrivelled purple the colour of alpen violet = cyclamen *fluttering like scattered moths*, I say to Ely, I mean that which is beyond contemplation, we withdrew to the library, then, and Ely embraced me with such passion that my left arm, which had come between our bodies, was not able to work itself free. The letters Ely wrote me, letters I kissed and stroked, as if my heart were leaping as if my very heart were itself being embraced, you see, more and more often we see it, yng. women baring 1 shoulder, it's seductive and it's foolish, I mean my feelings when I see them, they look especially seductive and foolish to me, they seem intent on baring their 1 naked shoulder to the breezes / the fragrance of narcissus and this makes them look both especially seductive and foolish (sometimes covered by a veil very likely made of crepe de chine, as Muzette or Mama called it, the kind of fabric they used to tailor sweet ltl. dresses for me, etc.)

in this slumbering state, out of this CREVASSE early in the morning, the heavens embraced, hazy (*dirty*) laundry thrown out beyond the horizon, and this delighted me because silent dim : draped = clouds accumulated. While 1 camellia, impromptu, '*after the distraction of a few hours*', Maurice Blanchot, had sown incorrectly, I say, I'm calling in all tools.

I've folded my hands and am sitting around in this leafy greenery. This year's summer, I mean 1 that flew past darted past, I say to Ely, from my window I have not caught sight of 1 single swallow while otherwise I saw them in mosquito-like swarms high in the blue, an infinity of swallows, I say, these friends of heaven and earth, you see. Who can possibly comprehend it, I say, why have they hidden themselves from me in this year's long but fleeting and *flitting* summer, why have they withheld their charms from me why, I say, why, I say, have they disappeared this summer and for good, why haven't they appeared to me this year, I ask myself, my fleeting *flitting* friends, darting heavenly wonders?

yesterday, early in the evening, after a generous rainfall 1 enormous double rainbow appeared in the east, I say, the 2nd rainbow was an outline, reflection of the first presumably, echo of the inner rainbow, which rang out so powerfully that it's chorales almost deafened me, while in the shadows of my thoughts '*the restless joy*' and so I relate to the appearance of a swallow in the same way I relate to the appearance of a theft, I mean, on the afternoon when we, Ely and I, in Café Dommayer and I, in the secluded part of the cafe gazing out into the garden restaurant, catch sight of 3 men seated at a round table, DISCUSSING BUSINESS OF SOME SORT, it also seemed to me as though I were being served an '*Egg in a Glass*', even though I cannot actually eat soft-cooked eggs, I say, I had pains of an uncertain nature and began *to contemplate*, and Ely asked, 'where are you?' actually I was sunk, *etc.* (the sml. teeth of the *etc.* are not actually relevant here, 'here in this musical farce')

through the JUDAS = peephole I observed the empty
corridor while in the carpeting I mean on the carpet
colourful sugar doughnuts I wished to sink my teeth
into, it was an abstract attraction, I say to Ely, an
abstract seduction, Muzette or Mama pointed to a pile
of excrement next to a brightly painted wall and because
they stopped and looked I thought the whole thing might
be 'chocolate ice-cream or choco ......'

as far as the consumption of meals at the sml. foldaway
table in the kitchen is concerned, it is all bound up in
some incomprehensible way with *a drive* out to one of the
suburbs where I am supposed discuss the poet G.R. at a
recording studio, I took the poppy seeds from the tablecloth and dropped them into the mushy vegetable soup
and then ate the vegetable soup so hot that burns on my
lips and tongue, *I mean the run of the world*

I don't know if I remember this or whether it is simply the
fantasy of a memory, I say to Ely, when I was 5, 1 of my
relatives carried me up to the Rax Alps on his back and I
remember crying because everything rocked, 1 of my
uncles, they called him ADI—2 or 3 decades later I was
walking down Anzensgruber Street with him when my hat
blew off : it was simply *blown off* and we ran down the
street after it. He asked, 'how long do you do it?', he was
referring to the time sexual intercourse with +++ took,
while my youngest aunt ('Herta') gave me roasted chicken,
SHE BUTTERED THIS CHICKEN UP and I scribbled off the edge
of my paper leaving traces of ink on my knee and calf, etc.,

no waist. I fold my hands and sit around in leafy greenery, *rain soaked rainy flowers*, 'motionless flowers' Jean Genet, 1 double rainbow arched over 1 page of my book, in a tender pearl-like hand, silhouetting the inner rainbow, apparently an irritation of the eye I say. I was perplexed when a stranger in the KONSUM market lay his hand over his heart and smiled at me—I was touched by this gesture but still wanted to escape it, I was not able to tolerate any approach of this sort any longer, I say to Ely, *in the sewing room* Muzette or Mama had begun to sew a sweet ltl. dress of etamine, I was 5 and kept insisting that IT WAS MY DRESSY DRESS because it had a pearl at the neck.

When we turn into our side street we always pass by a sml. ethnic restaurant, Ely once stopped there though uninviting, though an uninviting place, because he was unable to take even 1 more step (homeward), he collapsed into a chair, and thus rescued, we ordered (*course by course*) drinks and food. 1 *asterisk* in the night sky—I paused for a moment in the middle of the restaurant sensing what I believed to be a familiar scent, believed to have sensed it a number of years ago, though I couldn't quite place it, it shot through my entire body like a bolt of lightning, etc.

1 outrage, 1 wanton outrage, I say to Ely, to think I might start writing without inspiration, I was (am) *reclassified* as adolescent girl, I say, ('briefcase or school bag with a number of pockets') : we *stumble* around the city centre, Ely and I, 1 sailcloth bag in the display of luxury shop caught my attention, I put it over my shoulder in front the mirror and was shocked at *my title* : a monster (ugly)

with monstrous mail bag, repulsive, many tears, resulted in, upholstered, the fingernail on the index finger of my right hand, had actually split, and I, in order to prevent further incision, had wrapped it in gauze or HANSA BAND-AID, it had caught in the CONSONANTS of my creped hair, I say, I mean in the creped hairs of my head run wild, stuck between nail and nail bed, etc.

We were sitting at a sml. marble table in Café Tirolerhof and Reinhard D. bowed and kissed us with a heavenly smile that suggested he loved both of us.

my hands are folded and I am perched in leafy greenery

it wasn't really a memory it was a construct, an image, in which I saw myself as a painted figure, I saw myself *poured into* the garden meadow of a farmhouse : actually I saw myself in a photograph Ely had taken after we had fought with each other, and me crying uncontrollably, with swollen red eyelids sitting there in the garden behind the house, in the country. The picture of this female being, *poured out*, in a garden in a photograph pulled at my heart, it was a stranger sitting there poured out into a garden into a photograph with eyes cried red and swollen it was a stranger looking back at me : squinting back at me, hair as sunshade, etc., I may well have been sitting, slumped down, in a barley field surrounded by corn flowers and poppies, it was a colour photograph and the red swollen eyes among the swaying red poppy petals. We had fought the night before and my eyelids had swollen and grown inflamed overnight and you could see I had cried, my eyes small and inflamed I couldn't see very well I had to *squint* and was attempting to protect my eyes from the hot sun with my hands, my hands were a shield a cap (with awning). In truth I sympathized with the person in the photograph I mean I was able to identify with this person : she was sitting in a meadow full of flowers and butterflies and her sml. swollen eyes were squinting at me, it was, in truth, a so-called HOLIDAY PHOTO though nothing about it reminded 1 of happy days on holiday, it was actually a complaint—I was sitting slumped over there in a meadow in a garden in the country and I was holding my hands over my eyes as if to protect them as though there a cap with awning, and the figure was crying, still crying, or so it appeared, likely, *a wound*, actually this person appeared to be blaming herself, feeling guilty FOR HAVING STARTED the fight the argument, I mean, who did START this fight and would this fight never come to an end, it seemed it would not, I mean the sun shone, overflowing, as if gushing every last 1 of its tears. Actually (in truth) I was unrelenting and full of humility, I mean the garlic strudel I spread with butter and honey, intended for breakfast, the garlic strudel turned my stomach to such an extent that I had to throw up : the combination of garlic and honey was disgusting. And I held my head while I *was throwing up* the way Muzette or Mama used to when I was a child when they held my head, my forehead, as though they wanted to take my suffering away from me and assume it themselves—*and thus I was nesting in the mystical* my next book will be titled 'fleur', I say to Ely, (where all eyes are roses, Jean Genet), you see, his eyes were flowers, his eyes always looked like flowers to me, bluish grey silk flowers here and there in the meadows and hedgerows. The stylist Renée, *thinned out* I say, cleared the hair at my temples though already GROWN THIN—I shrank from the long razor she used a long razor and it was so sharp that at the very sight of it I felt pale and wounded, and we, Ely and I, roamed around singing loudly 'O dear God we praise you Lord we extol your strength the earth kneels down before you and hails your works' through the streets but our voices slipping away from us, in any case it didn't sound particularly Catholic, it was a kind of quick prayer, before going to my cardiologist's office. The dishtowel lay around in the kitchen, 1 yellow knot, full of a flood of tears, I took LASIX and my waters gushed out like a cataract, it keeps happening, I say to Ely, I find myself in a situation where I feel as though I am living in some aspect of my afterlife—but in all the colours of this life, so have I already truly experienced my afterlife and is it as true and familiar as the truest and most familiar this life? might it be a mirror image / reflection of this life here?

the string on the parquet floor *followed me everywhere* and finally knotted itself together like the fat body of an ugly black spider, I say, as far as frequent early summer visits to the Chinese restaurant ON are concerned, most of the time we sat inside bent over our WOK bowls using chopsticks = handling / beaking / *pecking away* reassuring each other how delicious the food, etc., as far as frequent visits to the Chinese restaurant ON are concerned, only once—

because the evening unusually hot and humid—do we
step out into the so-called GARDEN, actually a courtyard
planted with shrubs and trees which exuded a noticeable
cold and we could feel the dampness of the stone walkway
straight through the soles of our tennis shoes to our toes,
so we began to *rub them up against each other*, I mean *it was
all illusion*, etc.

Should we steal, go steal roses, Ely says, in order to have a
hostess present, but we hesitated to climb into the beds
and bushes and daggers, we didn't want to jam any of the
thorns into the tips of our fingers .. fresh as forget-me-
nots, I say to Ely, the way sml. umbrellas are opened over
the stands with postcards, hats and marionettes, set up in
front of shops (outdoors), in bad weather, you see, when
rain is expected, sweet panicles in the gloomy closet of our
living quarters, my refuge in *dawn's red glow*, the lilacs are
filling my senses, I mean, as far as the 1 single lilac bush,
on the corner of the street between the telephone booth
and an overgrown plot of grass, is concerned, I press up
against the lilac bush when I pass by but its fragrance
never reaches me, its fragrance perhaps too weak from
violet colouring to waft anywhere—probably wafted to
death?

it was an abstract attraction, I say to Ely, it might have
been a mosquito, Ely says : not a silverfish, it might have
been a mosquito, on the tile floor of the entryway, Ely
says, I mean by the bouquet in the vase on the tile floor in
the entryway, it might have been a mosquito suggested by

the fact that there is a lrg. bouquet of purple flowers in the entryway, flowers attract mosquitos, but I disagreed, etc., insisting that it must be a silverfish or a CENTIPEDE—the roses on the table were white, you see, actually they were yellow, they were yellow roses I mean *tea roses*, everybody calls them tea roses

as I was waking up, I say, it was there, *1 dripping sack*, in the east window and I cursed it, then it slowly transformed itself into an artificial white rose, under a pale awning, it TORE ME TO SHREDS, 1 night straight through to the marrow, I say, an unbearable glory or gloire, countless times racing past the hallway mirror to the toilet, forced to see that hour by hour I am ageing visibly, I don't even recognize myself any longer : the eyes my eyes slanting down as if being crucified, etc. I had been talking to Muzette or Mama and *her blackthorns* looking long and hard at me. 'Will accompany you 1 part of the way,' Ely says, and I composing a letter to a schizophrenic stranger who had written to me.

Leave it, just leave it! is the watchword, I say to Ely, and while the elderberries / monstrosities swaying in the summer winds, I with folded hands perching in leafy greenery, *in dawn's red glow*, I folded my hands and buried myself, tears streaming, in cushions smelling of wet leather, I clawed the cushions, 'monograms of ivy' and bits of thorn, Jean Genet says, *poppy seeds in my bed, in my 'Nordkette' clothing*, it was 1 abstract attraction : poppy seeds in my bed, in my 'Nordkette' clothing, etc., ltl. basket and calf at the window, immediately *in dawn's red glow*, I say to Ely, immediately wrote to the schizophrenic 'your letter = transformations, may you continue to find comfort and hope in literature', *1 co-op sweater*, Ely says, *this handwriting seems to be running amok*.

Crystal bird RAMEAU, it was 1 abstract attraction, I say to Ely, actually it was the 3 syllables (*'lovgreebo'*) and I recognized a friend's handwriting immediately, it was written on standard A4 paper with a green felt-tip pen and narrowly spaced lines held promise of a wondrous text, vitally important to me, but it turned out to be a dream and I was unable to decipher it, though written in my own hand, or so it seemed. So *please feed them the entire winter through* (Nina Retti) and who will, when she's dead, these sweet little woodland birds, I mean *nourish*, I say, she told me on the phone, *she's going to feed the sweet ltl. woodland birds the entire winter through*, etc.

On the phone Maria Lassnig : 'today I felt as though I was already roaming through my afterlife', but *who is going to feed them*, when she, Nina Retti, dies, I mean the great tits, who is going to feed them as SWEETLY in the lap of this HOUSE—everything in this kitchen is sticky : 1 halo 1 honey, 'bal' was honey in Turkish (thought-provoking film, 'spiritual realism'), and we've all survived another weekend, I say to Ely, *1 remarkable wreath of roses* / wreath of heart vessels undernourished, some kind of dance or hip-hop music, old worn waltz beat, on the radio, lay low the daring hopes of the morning, A BIG MOUTH simply attempting to compose the trail, so with the nail of my right thumb *made an attempt on* 1 of my tablets, made an attempt (to portion) to reduce it, I mean, and half of the tablet made a pirouette in the palm of my hand, and this amused us, Ely and me, you see. 1st snow waltz on my bread at breakfast, I mean it shot out through the curtains, I say to Ely, 1st damned tentacle of a heavenly fire, it screamed DUFY : THE DANUBE, the wilted petals of a wild rose dove into the depths of a full cup—

I went to the new chocolate shop on the main street *and down on my knees* got the only large round table, in the corner of the room, in all shades of pastel, bismarck-shaped BLOUSONS on a glass plate which in traditional *façon* balanced on a tall stem. I began to cry because this arrangement moved me and bewildered me, I didn't know .. it reminded me of my maternal grandparents' household, there were whole gardens of forsythia and *fontanelle* in the local cafe, I was always greeted *formally* when I went into the shop, this is why the stream of tears and I observed my tear-soaked face reflected in the marble tabletop, this loving exchange / love letters / passions of the sort where flowers are always being stolen purloined swiped, Jean Genet says *virtual = virtuous, I manoeuvred myself into this illness*, etc.

I folded my hands and flew up into the leafy greenery, *in dawn's red glow*, the blue tit : a poet's wording, in the Italian cafe 3 famous olive trees which were transplanted (apparently) from Orvieto—

in a heavy downpour as if I had said *in a heavy rain*, the woollen sheep, it was an abstract attraction, I say to Ely, as far as the large fluttering leaves of the fig tree at the

entrance to the garden restaurant are concerned, by the
end of the evening they had become objects of my yearning,
as had the serrated knife blade with which I into the deep
flesh of the nail bed of the middle finger of my left hand,
I mean with which I the middle finger of my left hand
almost completely (whereby the wound would take time
to scar over) and this still bringing tears to my eyes, I was
preparing a modest dinner on the folding table in my
kitchen, on which lay layer upon layer of old newspapers
instead of a tablecloth, you see, thus making the table
surface uneven and unsafe for preparations of any sort,
as it turns out, etc., and while handling the sharp vegetable knife my thoughts drifted off to that student of
poetry whom I believed myself not to know very well and
to whom *the aureole*, I mean the honours of my language
seem to disappear : reappear : only to disappear again and
I was not even master of it myself, and in the end, could
do nothing but *tremble* before it not able to intervene in
any way whatsoever, often robbing me of my sleep and
in the dark, nights on end, I roam through my living
quarters or favourite books, etc., and now after an
appointment with my cardiologist I stuff Ely's sweat-
soaked undershirt into my shoulder bag along with a
feeling of tender revulsion for the odour of perspiration
and its onrushing INFECTION, I mean all of this under the
sweet fronds of artificial glycinias in the doctor's office
and so I always stuff his sweaty undershirt into my
shoulder bag along with a feeling of revulsion that this
sweaty article will spread its odour and thus INFECT the
rest of the bag's contents, etc.

And while I, *the rags, shoving aside on the kitchen floor*,
contemplating my experience with this female personage
differing feelings arise, when e.g. I attempt to remember
what came to pass, the 1st time with her beneath the
shaggy crowns of the 3 olive trees in the restaurant garden
'Margareta', the 2nd time in the intimate interior rooms of
Café Tirolerhof, I say to Ely, everywhere this *brood of ants*
on tile floors, even on the rims of flowered cups at my feet,
and me on the edge of my bed, etc., my heart threatening a
standstill, you see, even though, 1 pure animal, you see,
even though, *1 animal in flowery crown*, even though, 1
hairy animal, in the WC, etc.

As if standing in front of a group of somewhat shaggy
olive trees, in which, and conversations of my friends
catching my attention distracting me, simply causing my
thoughts to disintegrate, like a deck of cards, then, you
see, with this female personage in the garden restaurant
'Margareta' the frostiness of the evening causing me to
shiver, the shaggy look of the 3 olive trees brought from
Orvieto and transplanted here, forced my tears, the whole
thing so distracting to me there simply was no exchange
of feeling or experience, this heightening my uncertainty
and distress, you see, and I got up and SPOKE with the
olive trees and oleander bordering the garden and their
branches seeming to reach out to me and in the end the
sugar-coated ROLL in the garbage can became infested
with worms, which like string, I mean, and Muzette or
Mama asked me if I knew what a *scabiosa* looked like, and
after some contemplation I answered yes : 'yes, with long
threads on its head and purple or deep blue in colour,'

and thus was overcome with a sense of happiness and contentment—it made me happy that I was able to clearly recall the flower that had accompanied me throughout my childhood in D. How is it that I am able see this flower so clearly now, in truth, this is an image recalled from the depths of my childhood, from my most distant childhood, and I simply shivered, I say to Ely, and I longed to *these incarnations* of scabiosa, the memory of these beds of scabiosa, embrace and kiss

I folded my hands and flew up into leafy greenery, *in dawn's red glow* this KIND OF WRITING is not simple, I say to Ely, because I write with my soul, I rub myself raw, I say to Ely, and I illuminate the darkest corners of this world, with my soul, my soul is a sml. flashlight, my soul is a sml. animal—it crabs around inside my chest and I can feel it crabbing, this might the 1st symptoms of an illness, my soul is on its way to composing on 4 legs, I say, it is crab-bing around my ribcage, going the distance.

Even though friends in the car are waving to me, speaking to me, I do not approach, I do not approach friends in the car, it's as though I'm planted, I do not approach the car in which my friends are sitting and speaking to me it's as though I'm crippled, keep my distance—why not go over!, my soul says, they're your friends, I stand rooted, a flag goes up inside my ribcage, 'so my revulsion and sadness' I say to Ely, 'even what is simulated truly' J.D. says, as far as the gallery, the stairway, the balustrade in that theatre are concerned, I say, it was almost *a loge catastrophe*, I mean

when E.S. overlooked the dark steps of the loge fell down
the stairway and over the balustrade with grt. determina-
tion, I mean CRASHED, etc., it was theatre catastrophe or a
stairway catastrophe, I say to Ely, *and almost everything
about this being wrong.* And as far this soul accident with my
friends in their car is concerned, they had rolled down the
window and stopped in my side street when they saw me
and the way I stood seeming to wait for someone or simply
stood : stood there, firmly rooted and *unconsciously* I began
to wave without approaching them as I if were afraid of my
friends, as if 1 incomprehensible fear were keeping me
from approaching them and thus the wave, warped smile,
(this contorted mask!) but still rooted, you see, the impos-
sibility of approaching them in their car and they having
rolled down the windows and begun speaking to me .. as
far as *my sense* of the word 'metronome' is concerned, it
has two different meanings, on the one hand it exists deep
within 1's ribcage, my ribcage, I say to Ely, on the other
hand it is simply the *reflection of the soul* of a poet friend of
mine (G.R.). As far as the 'metronome' deep within 1's
ribcage, my ribcage, is concerned, as it is irritating, frightening, a 'theatre catastrophe', 'stage catastrophe', 'stairway
catastrophe' *screaming*

'I'm hungry', I shout to Ely, 'give me something to eat,'
etc., scattered gladiolas, sml. swords, bouquets of iris, I
say, let's eat daisies, sorrel, tree ferns, lilac leaves, I hiss 1
banner, 1 symphony, I am suffering shortness of breath.

This grand recitative, = *gladiolas* on both sides of the large
green gate in D., and the nut trees too, I say to Ely, full of
these whispering leaves these LEAF CULTURES (Brittany), I

mean we rubbed the leaves between our fingers and they released an *overpowering* spiciness : ah a spiciness, I simply fainted, I say to Ely, the way I feel kissing, making love on the horizon, raining flowers, sweet singing flowers, no waist I mean.

So, in one (of my) bouts of *unconsciousness* I began writing this book, on 1 night in July, 1 o'clock in the morning, when I was unable to fall asleep, I say to Ely, when this bal-dachin of heavenly flowers crowned by a full moon and I beside myself, deafened by the fragrance of narcissus which from the hallway like waves from the sea pounding against my temples, you see, I had to WAKE UP and in my hands this bundle of soul, the stigmata of my devotion, etc.

I mean Ely and I through the park : Hartmann Park and a man was sitting there he was sitting on a bench and Ely said he's in shock (unconscious), head resting in his hands, *in a stunned state of mourning*, I mean he is mourning the loss of a friend a lover a dead child, you said 'stunned / unconscious' I say to Ely and I wrote it down.

Glide / slide, collecting gladiolas in a towel, these gladiolas : gatekeepers of summer, back then, in D., under starry skies, you see, as far as my gloves are concerned, at any one time I only 1 pair, strewn around like medicinal plantings, you see, on the linoleum floor of the entryway (the wardrobe) gloves and socks too and mittens, I mean early autumn—TRIMMING grasses, sun growing hazy, contemplating a parting summer (with sml. container got milk in a nearby village, 'and the milkman always in the vicinity of storm-like sounds,' Jean Genet says), RODDING and pond full of orchids, *fancied chocolate shop on the boulevard* or the milkman, recollection of foliage the milkman's in the garden restaurant in which the foliage : tongues of fig trees at the entrance to the garden restaurant (above shrubbery, of roots) the foliage of the fig trees my forehead caresses my forehead and my temples, and I find myself kissing E.S.' shoulders while the foliage of the fig trees at the entrance to the garden restaurant kissed my forehead and my temples, my hair—oh I could not fall asleep again it was already 3.30 in the morning, I had been lying awake for a number of hours, I say to Ely, eye position my eye position in the mirror in the hallway was *contorted*, contorted depressively, in such a way that I *was pursuing* the foliage of the fig trees at the entrance to the garden restaurant, I mean I was unable to sleep I was unable to fall asleep again—likely because deafening fragrance of the madonna lilies in the entryway was wafting in, I mean the fragrance flooded into my bedroom, across my bed me tossing and turning, etc., while the milkman : the breathless fragrance of the flowers in the entryway. It was actually true, the fragrance of the flowers on sweet wings had penetrated my bedroom, it was actually so that the seductive fragrance of the white lilies penetrating my bedroom had taken my breath away and I had to gasp for air ('thus the breathless text gasping for air', etc.), a voluminous book read through to the end, the glue holding the pages together was dripping onto my blanket, and the

leaves of the fig tree at the entrance to the garden restaurant, where my foot over protruding roots, *and me knuck-
ling down* working my way into the garden and I had
forbidden anyone from meeting me here, I say to Ely,
without calling first, just part of the ageing process it
seems. E.S. showed me how the propellers of her body =
vanes of a windmill, rotate, thus resolving physical tension in 1's chest, and my breathless body attempted to
copy the movement shown but the tension did dissipate,
at first, *who had gotten so wound up* about the wild roses
a.k.a. shrub roses, the 1's Muzette or Mama loved so
much. The leaf work of the fig tree trembled the way my
body does when it is suffering from shortness of breath,
etc., and the milkman played the role of usher in one of
the city's historical theatres, I mean he walked around the
parquet carrying a bundle of programs and *squinted* for
theatregoers ANGRILY for their seats (= Olaf Schilling). The
deafening fragrance of the white lilies swarmed deep into
my crown of roses, but there was no salvation

always practising daily routines while the dark pistil of the
white lily : of the new season, LACED me in, which forced
tears ('touched by grace'), and everything *gone mouldy* on
the balcony where Ely and I had spent most of the summer, gazing down into the crowns of massive trees tangled
up in trees of all different sorts, oaks intertwined with
shimmering overgrown lindens, even weeping willow
which down to the ground its trembling tendrils, you see,
I mean *polarized*, ETHICAL LIFE. I remember, I say to Ely, a

glycinia bush on a street corner in Rome enfolding me in
its branches when I approached it and touched its blue
umbels, it twined itself around me, my 1st visit to Rome,
its cloud of fragrance veiling = *my fluff, my nonsense*, my
eyes, my face—1 hand full or 1 mouth full of rose fragrance when I see the walled-up window : blind window
in the wall of the house where I was born and I tremble, I
have stumbled into the nettles of my passions again, the
shock so great that I put *1 of my hands* like a muzzle over
my *mouth*, as if this 1 sml. hand could hold everything
together, because otherwise my face in pieces I say to Ely.
The entire night tormented by a craving, thus cookies /
athletes in my mouth, tormented by hunger, not to be
quelled

oh my love my dear my dearest depravity, I shout to Ely,
before he leaves on his trip, 'I am trampling myself,' my
tattered text, I say, Muzette or Mama, back then, I say to
Ely, took her fur coat off, shabby in any case, and went to a
pawn shop ('Dorotheum') she took her fur coat off, her
stole, her ring, her brooch, knowing she wouldn't be able to
pawn them any longer, they were lost, her collier, her
necklace—*tautology*, I shout, I work in tautologies, I
shout, I work in tautologies, 'is dripping like milk from
an inexhaustible catastrophe', etc., of course instead of a
tablecloth I had the *barbed wire* of a cushion = migraines,
systemic, migraines / Mignon : that being something
sweet to eat, second upon second, while waking up, it
happens, I say, I find myself in Venice strolling across the

Rialto Bridge or leaping puddles on the pavement, because
overnight it had rained, and buy a souvenir for Ely (sml.
blue heart) but he won't accept it and gives it back to me,
we in the WHAT'S LEFT of all the puddles (on unfinished
wooden benches) sitting, together with Klaus R., but it
was too cold and I was shivering, everything was ALL
BUNCHED UP and Klaus R. looked at me with pale eyes I
have always loved. This *rhythm* : *this call of the Traun's
waves* always brings me to tears I mean I sat on the banks
of the Traun and cried over the allure of the Traun's
waves, it's my eyes, my eyes follow 1 certain wave, for
some seconds, before it disappears, and then they lock
onto the next 1, and 1 after that, accompanying them into
their disappearance, allure of a child (playing), perhaps. 1
wild rose bush : his, Klaus R.'s, revelations, when we,
Klaus R. and I in Café Central, and he aired secrets that
should not have been shared, I kept all of it to myself, I
owed him that, a friend I love and respect, shoulder blades
which always seek to be protected, time-lapse effect in
which the buds of the white lilies in the entryway begin
to open, the leafy passage of the glycinias (Genet), the
baring of the secrets of Klaus R., being transformed into
that rose bush over and over again, when we were sitting
in Café Central and he entrusted me with his secrets,
expecting me to keep them for all time, that night I folded
my hands unable to sleep, *and then I fell asleep*, wishing for
a SLEEPING BEAUTY SLEEP, a very deep sleep, you fall, deep,
deep, into a shaft or a fountain and you land in a meadow,
I say, with yellow daisies, surrounded by yellow daisies, I
say, a fairy tale texture or prospect, lying about like St
Florian, *in dawn's red glow*—

if a day goes by and we don't see each other, I say, I feel lonely, my shoes are full of water, I was sunk

...... like Tacitus

1 shred in a half sleep, I say to Ely, a flare up of prayers of thanks early in the morning, I dreamt you threw me out, my chirping character the Bolsheviks have thrown me out, in the soft green boulevards of my slumber, I say, *dark spots of pine*, I say, I am growing less and less tolerant of the 3 olive trees in the garden restaurant 'Margareta', I mean that the branches of the 3 olive trees in the garden restaurant 'Margareta' are growing more and more *thorny*, I mean I cry my eyes out being less and less tolerant as far as the 3 olive trees in the garden restaurant 'Margareta' are concerned, which are so knotty cracked *thornful*, have been said to have travelled a thornful way, as far as having their origin in Orvieto is concerned, you see.

It grew dim I mean my skull fundament grew dim, my heart hammered, no salvation, once I heard that voice on the radio, my tears gushed out in streams, I say to Ely, no single word regarding a laurel wreath in the photograph and in the foreground sml. flowers darting past : daughter Johanna in white banner—1 footnote 1 field mouse 1 fanaticism : Angelika K. said, she *hunted the mice down* in the grass, but they didn't get into the house

1 late Turner painting in the window, and it was over the course of 1 night that this aproned lower lip a lily bud opening up, it was over the course of 1 night that this

sentence was hatched, I say to Ely, it was over the course
of 1 night that I visit a number of families that *I* with a
number of FLEURS *I* am greeting you, I say to Ely, that on
my way home 1 beautiful shimmering green bug but it
didn't move, someone him, Ely, helped over a snow bank,
it was raspberry red, someone spewed raspberry jelly over
the slanted facade of the mansard window, I say, I saw
how they lifted you over the snow drifts, I say to Ely, but
the snow was raspberry red, as if I were viewing the world
though a pair of red glasses, *like a fiery red tongue of paint*
the thing stuck to the mansard window, leaked, moved
slowly downward, like snow drifts on a slanted roof, it was
over the course of 1 night that I *skirmished* with myself, I
lose a few drops running from the WC to the telephone
that had just begun to ring, while listening to Rameau,
that being gallant, all these bouquets of absent flowers, it
is a reverie, in my flowery hull in the attic room where I've
locked myself in, I say to Ely, it is a reverie, that we know,
Ely and I, it is A KIND OF PENITENTIAL, this motif of the
half-open balloon door or balcony door in Ischl, you see,
on the 1 hand this view of bristling combs = teeth of a
comb, of a howling forest in the uppermost regions of
mountains opposite I mean the bristling peaks / crowns of
a trembling stand of trees—on the other hand this *squinting* at damp stakes planted with grape vines, which surrounded the parking lot, in the left corner a sml. mulberry
tree, its branches bearing no fruit, are turning, waving,
wrapping, which is reverie, while consonant predators (in
Slavic languages) vowels bestially devour

he, Gerald B., was in the EMILIA, he said he was in the
Emilia, where he started out, unable to keep anything
down any longer, he ate every scheduled meal but simply
threw it all up, he ended up at the most sought-after location in the country and immersed himself in the warm
glow of southerly light, simply plunged into the warm
glow of southerly light, etc., and this taught him fevered
reverie (how to cry). After eating a meal he disappeared,
he disappeared a short time to vomit it up what he had
eaten, it was difficult for him to part from the meal he'd
consumed, it was IN SUNSHINE he disappeared and
returned having unburdened himself of the meal he had
enjoyed, *it was dark swatches of pine*, waist of his leg, the
squashed flat faeces of his body

and then I arrive, light of foot, dreaming, in stormy
weather nowhere near trees, once, I say to Brigitte St, a
person who always moved, but now a person who always
sits, lies down = I was once a person who moved but have
become a person who sits and lies down. Intending to :
imagining myself saying to 1 person or another, shouldn't
we be closer, but then, realizing this DESIRE not possible,
then consoling : above phallus of roots as if on spider legs
: extremely high-legged, remorseful, groomingly, guileless
appearing to be, a ltl. dizzy, and finally collapsing down
onto a wooden bench—so much weight dropping onto 1
single wooden bench before the forest visage of Wertheim
Park, or 1 of those scenes served up in the Turkish film
'Bal' me swaying in the forested heights of the treetops
(perhaps saddled)

as if I had actually found someone in Gmunden and then immediately lost that same person, I mean Emmy W., flying her way into the breakfast room of the hotel with wide-open arms, I say, even though uncertain whether it was her, because eyes still dim from sleep. etc., we promised each other, later in Vienna, we'd meet again in the Café and how we *glowed* at these promises—unrealized however, seeming to have forgotten to exchange phone numbers or for some other reason unclear to me, she pulled her lower eyelid down and one saw the red of her well-veined *eyeballs* like a throbbing *red glow of dawn*, or a throbbing red wreath of roses, oh the crustiness around the IRIS in the early morning of this *dawn's red glow* (entangling woodlands) in branches entangled found a photocopy of painting by Magritte 'Woman with Violet Face', I have always had ambivalent feelings about this picture, though, when holding this sheet up close my face always caught its fragrance—like the collage construct by Arnulf Rainer, actually composed using a photograph of my face, and mine the alabaster skin, I mean this NARCISSISM : cheek on cheek, and so I when approaching this poster on the wall wishing to touch the lips there. And I really don't understand why, I say to Ely, I don't really understand MUCH of anything because various unfathomable veiled context

who am I after all, I ask myself from time to time, what actually takes my breath away, makes me uncertain, no longer identical with myself, you see, and I don't really want anyone *with asterisk* : my skull to crush in order look inside, etc. (enraged werewolf)

this black sweat absorbing *skeleton costume* and me
(helpless) climbing the steps to CITY HALL / CITY REGISTRY :
when I married G.H. and flew down the steps of City Hall /
City Registry and my black sweat-absorbing skeleton
costume which had soaked up the odour and texture of
sweat, me throwing it into the surroundings, the groom's
violet face beamed I mean he was enchanted—

she, my hairdresser Renée is *identical with the way my hair
grows*, she knows how to work a ✂ through the *wilder-
ness* of my hair, I mean in which direction the roots of my
hair seek to be set / encouraged

THE SUN IS UTTER IDIOCY, etc.

(from a letter to E.S., 19 September 2010 : 'innermost
admired—feeling responsible that you are being imposed
upon from all sides, attempting to oblige you to take on
a number of things : in connection with me, I mean
"*dancings*", know these impositions have NOTHING to do
with me, they have not come from me at all, etc. even I
am being burdened in ways that are deafening and
unfathomable, and are not evident to me, etc., yesterday
saw the repeating repulsive *Sun Office* and also the
Swimming Pool by Edward Hopper in which the lifeguard
is attempting to cash in her hip injury, Ely and I have
however seen everything that is to be seen—and further
incantations / ruins, according to J.D. ...... ')

Gerund of early spring : as I was waking up

'*my innermost defiling*' and surface in flower honey (of the morning), Ely says, there will be a full moon, you see in a few days and I will the sea (the knife), and the way the full moon is reflected in the sea and the way the bougainvillea blossoms will entwine it, and the way I will race in its direction, I leant up against the open window and knew how my spirit would race to the full moon, at the moment of my death, I know how it will happen—I turned away and began to cry.

1 black-silk cassock, 1 sip of tea, 1 black-silk cassock over my body *smeared* with wildflower honey : *a bodily fright*. The foliage behind which the full moon was concealed for a moment *for a moment*, the head of the full moon embraced by the bougainvillea blossoms, many kisses, and Ely is lying (sleeping) next to me, across my chest at my side and Ely says, shouldn't we go back to sleep, I didn't know, had we actually slept together or had he (simply) slept at my side or had he (simply) slept across my chest all night

our somewhat fleshy nose, 'brittle, deliberate, serious, with your eyes somewhere else entirely,' Jean Genet says, 'with your eyes you are somewhere else entirely,' Ely says, 'where are you?', which was actually true, with my eyes (with my thoughts) I was somewhere else entirely. I was a LATE BLOOMER, I say to Ely, had *dreamy-cheeked* long life, the ltl. tips of the white violet. I thought it over I was terrified, someone might have broken in because I heard footsteps in the hallway, I saw the shadow of a shadow, I was uncertain, might have been Ely *finding his way in*, etc.

wildflower honey at my underarm, hanging gardens of my body, *luxury drawing* (reflection of the sun) on the kitchen floor, the old lilies in ugly *decay*, on the toilet, then, back at a memorial in the spring forests of Puchberg standing there in a Burberry (I was standing) and there was a goings-on of some sort or I was leaning up against a tree, tired, bored, and Ely gave me his hand to support me, he touched my hand but I was distracted ('scratching') through dark swabs of pine tar, etc. Dim sleep dripped out / ran out of my eyes while I often stumbling around the entryway at night—

the cat perhaps or the cranes at my feet, you see, it rubbed up against my knee, this phenomenon (occurrence), I say, it seems to me, he, Ely told me something about a cat when he called from Lentas (southern Crete) : it had simply shown up while we were talking and he whispered 'a cat' to me and I don't really remember whether or not he did mention a cat that had rubbed up against his knee but it was an illusion I mean the other day it seemed to me to be an illusion, etc. In any case, as far as this phenomenon (occurrence) is concerned, I found myself again, after being thrown off the train at Ely's departure and gushing tears forever—and what did all this have to with the cat that had rubbed up against his knee and THIS FLEET of cranes over a *restless sea* (*like a jewel I have been weaned*)

I wander and I walk, with bare feet, while I am reading in J.D.'s GLASS an event which occurred 2 or 3 years ago back into my consciousness, and me biting into a sandwich, angry because someone is speaking to me asking a question

and I am attempting to answer with a full mouth, imagining
my face misshapen by full cheeks, *I wander and I walk*, my
feet naked as *this fleet of cranes*, you see ...... you see
because the bookmark falling out of my favourite book,
falling out, falling to the floor, and then me not knowing
to which page I had read something which confuses,
angers, me, while Matthias F. says he took 1 of his
favourite books out of the bookshelf and the bookmark
fell out of this book to the floor, and he didn't know how
far he had read, etc., on the flat roof opposite *1 luxury tree*

(the inside of the upper lip CUT TO PIECES *by a milk tooth*)

then there was a freezing foot / *ploughing foot* at night,
though covered, domed with eiderdown, but I still felt the
arch of the cold wind blowing, you see. The whimpering
GREEN of unripe bananas, a fear of these *flowing* trees
sweeping up the stairway, driven on by a heavy storm,
while unflinchingly eyeing the day, I say to Ely, through
the spyhole (JUDAS hole), I say to Ely, on the phone, I can
see what's going on in the corridor, who comes and who
goes—by the light of day gleaming, I mean in the
tamarisks, I say, the tiny birds (like small silver balls on
Christmas trees), flittering. The rain has *torn the audience
to pieces*, it has torn the 'genêt' (means gorse) to pieces, I
mean the 1 with the sml. top on the crown of his head, I
want to be the sml. top = circumflex = on top of your head,
I say to Ely, on the phone, I mean on the crown of your
head, I say to Ely, he in a distant place. My black umbrella
(man's umbrella) is my prosthesis I have planted it :

embedded it in my WALK WORKS, in any case it should not make the sentences all too opaque, I mean, I say. I always need everywhere I need this *prosthetic altar* (Genet), SIDE TABLE where I can prepare things arrange things *ready things* = set things up put things up, because I of complex and corpulent nature, etc.

My thought or my *idea* falls like 1 pair of cherries from a tree under which you are standing, I say to Ely, I whisper to Ely, I mean with the apron which you are holding by its straps, and you are standing there with an open, wide open, bulging apron, apron at the ready like mine, like me, when I sit across from someone I love, and then my eyes are the receiving organ : I receive my lover through my eyes which torn wide open swallow devour everything (with a sob because my eyes, and my eyes grow moist)

when I fell in love with him, I say to E.S., I wrote him BODY LETTERS I mean I stuck body notes to his bare skin, but he never answered me—I stood in front of him in this *stammering inn*, approached him (to say goodbye) *his mouth* and he kissed me without passion yet ardently and long on *my mouth*, and while he kissed me I closed my eyes, was *soaring*, my body utterly released enveloped

'Miss St is a POET', *I was wearing my woolly tabernacle dress*, I say, and he burst into the neighbouring room with goat's leaf, etc.

Of course, 1 is COOL : a white scarf wrapped around my neck—flecks of sun on a ltl. wall like spotted cats, I first

saw the spotted cats on a ltl. wall, later flecks of sun,
couple of thrushes, I say, 'gauze wings, death' (Jean Genet).
This *eye longing*, my chirping bluebell, I say, couple of
thrushes, I say, and so much playfulness, entire sky falling
on my back (Jean Genet), been weaned, habit broken, like
a nursing infant, I mean. Then, back in Bad Ischl, I say,
along the 'cultivated' beds of the spa park the way we
tripped tripped along I mean under the piercing rays of
the midsummer sun again and again tripping into the beds
of the spa park in which the spa's FREE-FLOWING MILK spa
concerts had *gained great popularity*, or so it seems, as
we've heard, while we, Ely and I, strolling among cultivated
beds with peacock butterflies (moths and plantings), and I
wonder whether or not these peacock butterflies, these
plantings might actually possess some touch of charm or
are simply ostentation, I mean, were they ostentatious—
and me making notes with a MARKER = a felt-tip pen
colouring the balls of my hands black, blackening the
balls of my hands, the tips of my fingers, my nail beds, and
beds too, colossal ottomans, sofas, couches, hammocks,
recliners, and their snow-white covers then, when, I say,
we were in a *sunflower passageway* you see we were sitting
in the Rondeau Café of the Cobenzl observing the meadow
grasses that had been mown down by strong late summer
winds, *delightful* : *inflamed*, in the meadows surrounding
Café Rondeau of the Cobenzl, you see, down on their
knees these grasses stalks husks, I mean I followed their
movement, my eyes could not get enough of them = as we
say = of these wind catchers wind PAWS, of the fragile and
delicate flowers.

As far as the *smeared-up* sun is concerned, I drive it out
drive it away, I wipe it away with my hand as though
chasing off an obstinate insect : horse flies, hornets,
or the like.

On the floor next to his bed J.D.'s elegy for Emmanuel
Lévinas, whose face on the book cover appears to be
getting paler by the day, his freckled ear, excrement thin
as a thread, scholarly bloom, *eyes seeking*—

oh you embankments of love, my elegiac nature, I say to
Ely, it happened then, back then, for 1 moment, for 1
tender moment his eye caught mine, it was like a bolt of
lightning, but we did not acknowledge each other, it was
then with ++++++, you see, it actually did happen to me
with ++++++, it was 1 single bolt of lightning, it was 1
single moment, his eye caught mine, in 'Museum of the
20th Century', actually many years ago, I say to Ely, it
touched my heart, it was electrifying, I say, these gusts
of winds buffeting me are very lonely, I say to Ely, this
channel these emotions and as I am writing these words
down, *my hands stretching into the air*, are these illusions
(these lilies), I mean, such a shrt. letter : such a shrt. note
toilet paper

like a cow licking salt from the flat hand of the herder my
PASSION licks word for word from the library of my
favourite books, such *caressing poesy*—

as far as glacial ice is concerned I mean as far as ETERNAL
ICE is concerned, I say to Ely, it starts melting ('the hot

breath of a child!'), it melts and is transformed into ETER-
NAL TEARS, I say to Ely, I see myself in a photograph taken
a number of years ago very thin on the *Pasterze* standing,
you next to me, I say to Ely, do you remember, we were
standing in front of the Glockner Massif, an eternal semi-
nar, etc., calling to mind as I woke up the way I slobbered :
overburdened by love, having to think about 1 certain
person, overburdened with love, I say, hours later
ashamed of my feelings which had simply TAKEN THEIR
COURSE in the meantime, perhaps never even having
existed, e.g. shrilly in my innermost being the question
could I actually cry for this dumb round *scruffy* visage =
my own, so looking down on my own dumb round scruffy
visage would I be able to cry : gush tears. Thus the desperate prayers at night, unable to sleep, I say, these desperate
prayers for sleep soon for soon sinking into a state of
sweet unconsciousness, a no longer knowing of place or
time or person—I mean including this mirrored existence
of the dream me sitting in late summer in a streetside cafe
and seeing a person approach *approaching me*: and me
uncertain whether I knew her or not as her heavy old face
transformed itself within seconds back into a slim youth-
ful face, I knew well, me utterly and completely unsettled,
then, I simply leapt up and embraced this person without
being able to remember her name

me isolated, in these gusts of wind, I say to Ely, gradually
conscious gradually waking up or early in the morning
after waking up slobbering from love, I mean slobbering

longing for love, afraid always : innermost *pasted*, even
early morning, I say, I mean something cursory between
the words : a tachisme among my words, ink on my fingers
and on my words, real trails, I can actually see it right in
front of my eyes, ink trailings trailing off black inscription
(crown) ribbons / and we, Ely and I, not knowing how we
were going from Gumpoldskirchen : from the cemetery at
Gumpoldskirchen (where my parents are buried) not
knowing how we were going to get back to the city, trains
rarely (seldom) even they tachistic tailings trailings plaits
fleeing and ravines, Arnulf Rainer's black ribbons of ink—
when 1 ink / inks oneself, the tips of 1's fingers, 1's finger-
tips with runny ink, black or purple, like PAINTINGS of
night-time skies when at night stumbling through 1's
housing to the only window : *feet dragging* and outside
night-time Violas = bluish black / purple heavens, 1
lament, 1 shivering loneliness, I mean Arnulf Rainer's
Trailings, the heavens with ink running overgrown
silenced, 1 single trumpet blast, I say, 1 single black trumpet blast, you see, the night-time heavens 1 black tail,
when at night approaching the only window in this silent
black loneliness, wreath-ribboned night, wafting across
the horizon, etc. The night sky this clotted blood, this
nightly catastrophe, forest catastrophe, still not knowing
whether the forest zone is purple or black, you see, *the
inclination of the night*, the night inclines to morning, but
absence of sleep, (or in order to free oneself like 1 STRING
OF SNOT / ROBIN REDBREAST, I say, but with hands full of
flowers (Genet), roseau = stick perhaps rose tree—they
had tilled everything, but after 5 weeks had begun to work

the soil again, plantings were 'common' / ordinary lysanthus, the kind Ely had always loved preferring them to any other kind of flower, etc.

And so a cloud dressed me in the morning as I woke up, I say to Ely, my blister filled and my stomach wanted to turn itself inside out, the way one feels before throwing up, but I had nothing I would have been able to churn out, my stomach empty (applying the standard one applies to rats—'thou shalt not kill')

1 tearing away, 1 being torn away by someone, I say to Ely, have no spine, BEING A WORM, I say, crawling around, sliming around—born to be an agave and then march : march into the unknown world, I mean as far as these arched curving trembling young trees are concerned, along the avenues of the *Stolbergasse* they are *in leaf* THROUGHOUT THE YEAR, they are so extraordinarily leafy and hardy they seem to be enveloped in densest song

crying I picked up scattered chunks of sugar from the kitchen floor or crying I sweep up scattered sugar cubes, the empty bags, foil wrappers, crumpled red napkins— everything here sticky with honey : pens, notepaper, Henkel glass, cow chewing its cud ......

not the scenes I remember, rather the *sensations* accompanying those scenes, I say to Ely, I mean relaxed under the bristling (thorny) olive trees in the garden restaurant 'Margareta', then, with Bernadette H., and me beginning to collapse and finally nothing more : truly NOTHING

MORE to think : to say, *under flowery calyx slumbered*—
(likely inside flowery calyx) it was an abstract attraction, I
say, while dogs flattered me, etc.

'you are like the Saviour with his sheep', I say to my doctor,
when 1 of them gets lost in the underbrush you call for it
and free it from the hedges, if 1 of them dies in a gorge, you
climb down to get it, etc. In the morning, Ely says on the
phone, the sheep cross the mountains to attend Mass in a
neighbouring village, I can see them from 1 of my windows,
warmth is most important, contacts are most important,
Ely says, the thorns in Crete's hedgerows, they make me
bleed, mornings the herd crosses the mountains, BLEEDING,
they get caught in the thorns, I've been caught in the
thorns, I say to Ely, the idea of me as beggar is 1 I will
keep and nurture (Jean Genet). Then, I say to Ely, I was so
in love with ++++++ that I got down on my knees to *mop
up* his vomit but a sticky residue remained—like the
kitchen floor in my living quarters where everything sticks
and crunches when crossing in rubber soles—I was
CRAZY about ++++++ I was ready to do everything for
him and to forgive everything, he pressed me up against
the wall and tried to kiss me on the mouth and desire
flooded through me : I threw my arms around him. It was
in the *folio room* and we were unprotected, we might have
been interrupted and surprised anytime by anyone, from
time to time he mentioned LULLS but I didn't understand
had no understanding, and so he started serving up our
memories on a tray along with roasted dove, you see,
these veiled trumpet trees in the garden restaurant
'Margareta', large fig leaves resting on our foreheads

cheeks and lips, and as soon as we stepped out onto the moss-covered steps we both began to cry, I saw the way his eyes began to roll, to move back and forth, these eye-balls in speechless awe, etc.

As far as the time I lost my way at the airport is con-cerned, I simply started running in this direction and then that, and finally Ely and me : you see, he threw his arms into the air and called out my name, finding me on this pale evening, and me crushed ground to pieces collapsing—fainting spells, racing laced shoes, magical scraps of foil wrappers in the early morning, I say, 2 sml. spoons in a cup, using 1 empty open drawer as a table, 1 rushing pair of underpants, choking episodes at breakfast, hoping somehow to hold time up / hold it back / bring it to a stop, firmly clawing into its mane, and then I hold my own cheek then I wrap my own lips and then seeming to be dead, every time I enter the supermarket I'm touched. In three parts in the labyrinths of the forest, you see, and me crushing the flowers, 1 incantation : 1 tenderly hyster-ical woman, I say, I kept losing the ground under my feet, 'it's my Saint's Day', J.D. writes, I fold my hands and fly up into the leafy greenery, and everything I am writing now is probably FOLDED : something folded, 1 folded cloth coat the kind I wore at elementary school, scattering butter-cups on the street corner, a pissoir like St Florian *in dawn's red glow*, DUCHAMP coltsfoot leaves a meadowland : *Archangels Spitting to Him*

As far as the relationship with Bernadette H. is concerned, I say to Ely, it was frightening and we sat in the *pleasure gardens* of the restaurant 'Margareta' and I could feel my figure growing more and more devoted and finally sinking to the ground underneath my chair, my old woman unready to inhabit the *pleasures* of my own writing and dissonance poisoned my consciousness and despair brought me to tears—and me pawing my feet feeling the need to leave this garden immediately, the fragility of the rose bush in the entryway, I say to Ely, surrounded by swarms of mosquitos and from 1 day to the next threatening a fall, I leapt in, I bent down to him, the rose bush and lovingly dug through his wild if frail splendour many dishtowels on my sml. typewriter table, the archangels spitting to him. It is, you see, a kind of *flower tree* and it appears this tree, these 3 Giotto Trees are : lilac bushes and bird trees, especially the youngest most delicate Giotto Tree seems to be 1 grape vine, it has no leaves only umbels of wine grapes : lilac umbels and Francis of Assisi is preaching to the birds under this Giotto Tree, and they pecked at his bare feet, they listened to Francis of Assisi's sermon : 'and there I fell upon a feast for my eyes, standing before this budding hyacinth dove .. through the night Magnolias .. '

what we have here is 2 sml. spoons in a cup—RITZERFELD (Helene) as the publisher introduces herself. Like a giant dog : the way this giant dog like a giant bear on the divan in the office Literature House as C.F. told me the way the bowls of this giant dog were standing in front of the office door of the Literature House, you see, a fur collar for this old giant meant to encourage him to move, *things were heating up* early in the morning, something or other was simmering, my cousin telling me he was almost deaf, no longer able to hear the *soulful* tones of the television set, but could follow the pictures on the screen, etc.

The doctoral candidate like Prince Ironheart, C.F. says, I will STEAM myself in my throat, a man came up to me and stopped, I say to Ely, laughed at me and reached for my hand *as though he were a thief.* He robbed me of my hand he grabbed at my hand as if he were grabbing for a trout under water, I didn't know him, I was stunned, I might for 1 second or so have mistaken him for a musicologist from the local radio station, I smiled at him in my fright. Everything grows hard, I say to Ely, like my aversion to Mozart, I say, other things achieve clarity, I say, like my love of Bach, everything so PENETRATING on the 1 hand, everything so breathtaking on the other, as we grow older growing hard : growing stiff, all of us simply better off striving for wonder and clarity and beauty, *budding Giotto Trees* ......

Juices, lamb, this buffeting, because fitting me good cheer because defying myself in good cheer, a book lay open in front of me, I say, image of trembling branches in the air straight through me. Since the beginning of the year living in idleness, I say to Ely, pollen (more than iris), and then had a dream about two film actresses, I say, with flat headgear made of cardboard wearing DOLL'S DRESS. Me lying awake in butterfly way because with a sand clock and rings around my eyes, I say, because, you see, with the sun *broken out*, me having to squint, with Dufy's Window Shutters, I say, with themes of slowness, powerful kisses ('you are a master of kissing'), I say to ++++++ as he drew to him and kissed, he kissed me on the mouth and it was an eternity, soft and eternal, and I didn't move. 'Are we an exalted pair?' I ask him.

Just sitting around here GRUESOMELY now and blood is steaming, I say, made a sketch on paper now that Ely is back home from Crete, fold my hands and fly up into the *leafy greenery*, etc., my glasses diamonds tickets in the WC, I mean the bougainvillea from Crete, Ely says, and he takes me in his arms, Sonja H. has a boy, inconceivable, I say to Ely, C.F. is a window creature with a set of keys and an ice-cream cone, the ice-cream shop on the corner closed since yesterday, palms borrowed from a local restaurant rolled back to the flower shop (wooden flat with wheels) the bathing sock in the Red Sea, I say, evenings with waves and FLORA can feel it but still do not understand it this imminent end, I make my way to the restaurant, long, it is 1 long way (through Hartmann Park)

in Puchberg they say, where all the time *thud of rain*, now, glancing towards the window rain fall beating down extraordi-narily loud, we trudge into the forest, marking trails with high boots, softened up, you see, or, these texts, he says, like an abstract painting, e.g. me frightened out of my sleep at 3 o'clock in the morning, by the cry of the snow of a bird : hood over the floor lamp next to the bed, the giant plane trees at the balcony (= rustling gazelles or brothers), I dive down into the leaves, their leaves touch me, —repeated beginning and keeping every 1 of my variations, I say, the leaves of both plane trees in front of the balcony appear to be moving they appear to be SMASHING, on delicate stems the trembling leaves, *butterflies fluttering*, I mean on the lower trunk the trembling leaves on their delicate stalks and opening up like butterflies, and the silent birds in the foliage, as far as the disfigurement of age is concerned, I say to Ely, this wobbly end of a sentence no one really understands

in the middle of the underbrush 1 tall red tulip in full bloom on the balcony across the way, I say to Ely, something or other red Spanish red in the corner of the room, I say red stocking or 1 scrap of postal scroll rose-red twilight but the scrap was screaming, I mean the red rags ties ribbons and masks, he was covered in red silk, glowing red butterfly ruby-red butterfly 1 branch from linden tree torn off and bleeding, giant tail or *fleet of swallows* : 1 EYE LONGING : 1 book lay open in front me—this breath these breaths, was not actually aware of myself, I say, was standing at the sink these ltl. notes ltl. letters ltl. folded papillons of toilet paper, English was his, Ely's 2nd native language and thus *his Feverish Novel*, you see, I say to E.S., rosehips rosemary rosarium in the supermarket, grown fond of paper bags, always have a paper bag with me wherever I go, I say, put a handful of sugar cubes in a sml. bowl while hare was in the hallway window I mean early in the morning as I was

eating breakfast and using sugar cubes as PRETEXT even
though handful of sugar cubes (*kicking*) falling to the floor
and me with the tip of my foot kicking them under the
cupboard (*and kicking*) oh Chinese bride she gave me a
Chinese tablecloth still wrapped in white tissue paper on
the folding chair under my kitchen table, of snow-white
damask it rustles whenever I touch it—I mean *looking
into the heart of emancipation*, radically, he says, you look
very rustic, we are sitting on the Danube, we travelled to
Budapest, we visit the Jewish Quarter, I wearing a
parka, the cabbage white at his temples, he says, we're
not lovers, etc.

We are concerned with *tone* : the colour the hat and I
arriving late for the Bielefeld Colloquium, you see, the
colour blue : a faded blue, or jeans, arriving late you see,
panting up the rise to Neuland House, go to a woodland
pub because I'm hungry, turning left to the woodland pub
it being a matter of tone very pale a pale blue—delayed
arrival having transformed itself into a colour, faded blue
the cap the pants the mountain. What occurred to me
then, and was already noted down on a notepad, my fingers are always green because I write with a green felt-tip
pen, 1 sml. pile of butterflies on the parquet, I pick BERRY
BY BERRY from the hedgerows and native plants along the
way, Ely says, and me about to lose my way to a friend's
house a long way away in a far district (Reinhold Posch), it
was *pollen* it was an illness and we let the curtains down so
that the melancholy 1 covered us only in part, you see, the
melancholy 1 touched us only with her lower branches—
oh the phallic roots the grasses on her furred pathway, my

step shaky my eye unsteady, so I fold my hands and fly up
into the branches

am a traitorous nature, 1 laming rigour

am *touched by deafness* no longer hear the peep of the elec-
tronic thermometer, I fax Klaus S., would like to know
how you are, etc., listening to Bach's Hunting Cantata
'Sheep May Safely Graze', clouded horizon, embrace the
world, *dunked* the JOSEPHSTADT into a glass of water, it is
more attractive, just inserted a photograph into the text,
am handicapped with stormy attitude, I say, crazy red
when suffering migraine, I mean deafening red in a glass
in the meadow, this *pollen* I carry in a black plaited bag
slung over my shoulder—glancing high into the crowns of
these trees in the garden, seen from the balcony, where
me huddled up in a wicker chair in the shade

*('Otto put his arms around me and pulled me to his chest but
his handwriting was ripped away .. ')*

someone was there just now and told me about the *pollen*
of forget-me-nots eyes of Muzette or Mama, it was just in
passing or during the dance parade someone told me
something about the *pollen* in the eyes of forget-me-nots
to either Muzette or Mama, I mean, these forget-me-not
eyes to ashes already to ashes a long time ago ashes. Oh
she was so TIRED OF IT having to listen to the endless
complaints of her patients that she started opening and
closing the desk drawer, she was edgy, kept opening and
closing the drawer and even started telling her patients

about her own problems, or waited for a humorous
remark from her patients or *jumped up* and *leapt* into the
kitchen for a cup of tea or *leapt* to the telephone to make a
call thus achieving distraction because no longer able to
tolerate the complaints of her patients, etc.

in the midst of the underbrush she could no longer hear the
peeping of the digital thermometer, the building's doorbell
ringing, a friend whispering on the telephone, the voices
of actors on stage

I wake up among 'cultured animals', I once lay in a baptismal font I am unable to remember whether I was ever
baptized the word 'baptize / baptized' *drifting down to me*,
winter baptized us with snowflakes and brooms and
waterfalls of tears frozen to our cheeks, I say to Ely, they
drifted down on me like baptismal water before freezing
into ice, I say, and now I look into the mirror and I am not
self-assured, I am suffering, I say, my tears freeze, and
Christiane Z. gave me a muff, it smells like tobacco, somewhat out of fashion, Christiane Z. says, I have never possessed a muff, muff possessed. 'The horse or the flower no
longer takes to its heels like Giacometti's dog'—Christiane
Z.'s sml. dog on the Brigettenau bridge or spur, where the
Danube Canal branches off from the main river which
itself runs back to mosses pheasants wings tree ferns
(much loved by Muzette or Mama) : she loved ferns most
of all. In the morning at the beginning of the new week, I
mean *on the 1st weekday* feel so liberated and *renewed*, I
say to Ely, because the stores I frequent most of the time,

now open again, 'in unison humming'—the chocolate shop e.g. which on the weekend the sign FERMÉ on the door I mean signifying a shop INACTIVE, etc.

You see, in the cool half shade of your character, I say to Ely, when you, exhausted from work, in the late evening, hardly respond, your cautious silence I mean, whenever I ask anything or confess (my misery), but you still healing my wound and I will suddenly start reading around IN HEGEL, paws of Christiane Z.'s dog spread (slime up cover up) with acacia honey

on the balls of my left hand buttery honey POLAND, 'the well-buttered country POLAND', J.D., where 40 years ago a palm reader approached me wanting to read my palm, finally I relented, but not without trepidation, I say, she prophesied 'long life and loneliness'

with a feeling of unease I saw that my favourite reading (GLASS) was dwindling, and thus, well aware that the end of my favourite book was near, was facing the prospect of having to begin reading this book again, how many times had I done this?

in a corner / cover of the room *the mountain feeling* : I write to Peter Waterhouse 'one has to read your new book very early in the morning after a less = almost sleepless night, after having evacuated one's bowels (crude) while insides still trembling and shaking,' SUPPLENESS NIGHTINGALE, etc.

I found the wording pleasing 'I had blackened him up,' but I didn't know which person I was referring to—1 younger stranger, a youngish woman approached me with pen and paper in the cemetery and asked for my autograph, I say to Ely, I had a problem on the peak of the mountain in I., have a tendency to forget about him = Ely, I say to Muzette or Mama, have a man from Calabrese on my mind, I say, am making helpless attempts to read the clock at night, now stop more often along my favourite walks, look back, much haziness at twilight (fog), still much shoots / flashes through like a bolt of lightning and then I see everything clearly, I start speaking to a stranger in the tavern 'do you remember 1 Marian Feast Day you were standing in front of St Thekla's Church, on main street, holding a white lily in your hand and you gave me the white lily and then I went into a shoe store but the GRUMPY old dog wasn't there he might have died, *he was suddenly pale*'

I've become religious, I say to Ely, 'one of
the disciples lay at
Jesus' side, it was John
whom Jesus loved ....he leant
over to the chest of
Jesus and said ...... that he (Jesus)
did not really want to
sleep with a woman
I understood (at a
certain place) ...... a cloth
lay folded next to them
at a certain place I
will battle them with the sword
of my mouth I
hunger for John ......'

the white petals of the rose lay on the floor strewn across
the floor of my bedroom I say to Ely, and as I had begun
thinking about Café Prückel at night, I cried, because of
one strand of my father's white hair on an upholstered
chair many years ago : he went to the Café every morning,
etc. At night I looked at the wall mirror and caught sight
of my DISINHERITED face. *I had vanquished Phoebus.*

A landscape not to be travelled, I say, 'this subordinate
tiger,' I said, and looked the Chinese pianist in the eyes, I
looked into an old face that moved me, it attracted me in
its gentleness and I kissed it before the subordinate tiger
could attack me and the whole glass-smooth parquet of
the dance hall of the auditorium of the Academy of

Sciences would be covered in blood, and if I am unwilling
for these events to come to pass, because I am exhausted,
I say, I will cross her, the way Raoul Dufy instructs, with
fine level strokes of my pencil cross her out, I am a Fauvist
of language, perhaps a Dufy of Alpine ranges, I say, with
papillon in my hair among the strands of my hair, 'falls
fell', writes Peter Waterhouse, and thick of hair and
shoulder bones—

just sitting around here gruesomely now, being driven carried
off and blinded by visions, I say, this bud here and this
shop with the pelts in Perchtoldsdorf, I say, with fox wolf
raccoon tiger and hare, and in the middle of it all this cafe
where in the atrium in summer under lianas ivy and grape
vines, you see, always shivering because the atrium in
the shade, etc. As far as the musculature of a tongue /
language is concerned, I say, at 1 time I suddenly lost /
forgot this musculature, I was unable to even move my
tongue, my words were all lost, *a fake* e.g. I showered him
with fakes, estranging him, he rejected my fakery, he flung
the fakery right back at me he was outraged angry, leaving
the WC I had a chocolate finger or what looked like 1, I say
to Ely, I want to become *an unbridled classicist*, I stood at
the border of the meadow full of thorns design or Dasein
while the rusty razor of the sun, this being the secret, I
am out of fashion, I say to Ely, his Alpine visage burnt,
the photograph showed a swaying tearing GRIZZLING face 1
simply had to love—these cherries on the trees actually
cherry blossoms thus signs of the cross, Dufy's trees like

4-leaf or 5-leaf clover, I say, 1 winter glove with 3 fingers =
1 incantation, 1 yellow console next to a bouquet in a vase
on a small table in Dufy's atelier (with red ribbon)

my dreams stuffed full of buttercups.

Having to forget the feathered fruits of 1 poet before I am
able to consume the fierce fruits of the other : P.W. / J.D.,
that they might nourish me, am extravagantly stingy, I
say, need much space much time much money, etc. Then,
there was a RISE : SERPENTINE RISE on a garden path covered with gravel, me conjuring it up, actually sensing my
steps again, in my ears / my breath, a muted sound, you
see, after so many years

in our senility the reversion of our sex organs to excretory
organs, *and was gradually able to speak,*

onto my black hairstyle *sml. leaves* or the like (embroidered), even as awake wondering if I might actually be
able to repeat it and with C.T. through Roman streets
which billowed like purple banners and at the entrance to
a church the English words 'say po-po' and us surprised,
giggled and *dunking* 1 display in rose-coloured hues was
led to observe : 'just like children' *and me seeming to come
to a halt* in this magic like a factory or a motor—was very
guarded or quenched sunk deep into this state of sleep
and dreaming through magical touch in a deep peace as if
a deep peace had released me, and me asking myself if I
might have to go on living in a corner / winter sleep and
without friendship and without joy in mobility and I

caught sight of a pair of eyes : pairs of eyes of a swarm
of children sitting upright at their desks, pairs of eyes all
different, many of those were narrowly spaced and others
were widely spaced, each 1 of them inspired.

He, Ely, opened the doors FEARLESSLY, a starting pistol
hidden behind his back, the burglar retreated
immediately—

mornings hunger brought me to the breakfast table
which had been ornamented with the bakery of the day
or embroidered with the sml. leaves of the day on the
tablecloth, it might have been holy day but I had brought
my bad conscience with me, I passed chocolate cookies
around, *the garlands of my handicap*, etc., I folded my
hands and flew up into the leafy greenery. The weather
was numbered, the bread seller handed me my piece of
bread with a beatific smile, and I smiled back, the seedless
grapes I had bought in the supermarket were wet and
black in places : like a cobra. My father wore American
suspenders that kept the waist of his pants at his chest, I
knew that about Ely when he was young, I loved that
about him—it was his HOUSE-FATHER ATTITUDE, he slept
naked, but I never saw him walking around naked he
always wrapped a sheet around his body making himself
all the more attractive. The conversation fell to me,
through intellect, I was alone in the world : it was (like) a
snow driven a rubbish talk, I even embroidered at the
beach, ltl. leaves of the day above the waves, sometimes
between the waves (like) notes writing, I gave presents of
things I would have liked for myself, it was in my character
to carry the full can of milk through the rain, *Petrarca*

asked me if I liked Dufy. The papillons among my shoulder
bones, my rib cage a little white broad and deep (from
stag), the direction the bullet flies, I say, deer system
racing past, Elke Erb says, Dufy's Fauvism, will have to
admit I am distrustful actually Argentinian, and sensitive
(according to Dostoevski) the less 1 knows, the more 1
suffers,' these churning snakes and intestines, I say to Ely,
these magnolias : night-time hours, most typed events,
this forest-floor visage, THIS PURE HEART. My father
threw his silverware away once he had eaten he threw his
silverware onto an empty plate, after eating a meal he
threw his silverware away, he threw his silverware onto
an empty plate, leant back, etc.

so that my knees form a table, in bed

you tear me out of my contemplation, I say to Ely, the
fragility of a bouquet of roses ...... the illusion of a lily in
form of bunches and gusts of wind

I remember, we, Ely and I, sat *around the corner* in the
shade while our friends sat *around the corner* in the sun I
mean it was a coffee-house garden that had 2 sides and 1
side stood in the shade (where we sat) and the other side
was in the sun directly on Francisco Square—and the cafe
was actually named 'ltl. Café' and it actually was small, it
didn't have many tables indoors it had more tables outdoors, directly on Francisco Square in the sun and *around
the corner* in the shade, the ravines and streets around us
were still in full flower at 2 in the morning when I woke up
no longer knowing who had offered me his full glass

across the table for a toast the previous evening, I forgot
our friends' names, at the concert in the spa park in I.
enormous winter roses (in midsummer) and as we milled
around in beds of winter roses we wished them swollen
red as they were white, and trampling them trampling
them in love, bedwards while swans, most separated in
heart, Höld., how strange, I say to Ely, 1 entire day
believing in happiness and the chortling sanctity of
laughter, I say, and it really only lasted 1 day, I say, and
then slipped back into this wistful melancholy, and I was
content. I have never had Rhetoric, I say, with all the
Flowers and Decorations, never Rhetoric, only aspired to,
he kissed the ankle of my left foot and stroked it, then,
the Archangels spit into him, Genet.

Lost in thought *about a lad at the seashore* or bushes, and
1 hedge full of chirping finches sparrows and humming-
birds, o there were bushes full of concerts *and discovering
Glory*—I'll be going to the Essl Museum, Ely says, and I
reply, 'it is something I have always wanted to do, etc.'

the sml. sad *scraps of a wild stream* on the kitchen floor
and tears came to my eyes when I called her and asked if
I were interrupting, she said no, but a few minutes later
she said she had a guest, etc. In the morning I recall
flickering tears and dreams of the night past : worms in
my pasta, long underground passages in a cellar, my own
breathing, opened my eyes at 5 o'clock in the morning.
K.S. defended herself in this argument with bull-headed
eyes, it frightened me—I ran my finger over Ely's eyes on
the cover of the book I was holding in my lap, Ely's friend,
Ely's sad considerate thoughtful eyes, I started to cry, I

knew those eyes, nothing ever escaped them, I ran my
finger over the eyes behind his glasses, it seemed to be
1 signal, 1 fetish.

As for the thick plumage and quills on Ely's flying hand in
the photo, it swirled white and heavy through the air, his,
Ely's visage almost masked, after making up with Ely there
were screams, cries and shouts perhaps a thundering
Christmas, perhaps I had misheard what was said—

and EvS gave a ltl. speech in the room where our visitors
had gathered it was raining outdoors *darkening*, someone
was here with a sml. dog, and it whined throughout EvS'
speech, I squatted on the stone floor of our little room
because I was unable to stand any longer, our visitors
stood in a circle listening to EvS' speech and not letting
me out of their sight. I remembered, I say, we were sitting
in a CAFE and I was afraid I would have to visit R.D., I
was afraid I would have to say something there, what
should I say, I had nothing to say, I didn't want to say
anything at all, all I wanted was to sit at home and read
and take notes and by reading and taking notes find
inspiration for my own writing, it often took no more
than 1 word, 1 line, 1 paragraph to find inspiration, I said,
when I cough I most often cough up phlegm, something I
hadn't done before, I had never coughed up phlegm
before, as I was waking up, I felt a pain shoot through my
right shoulder blade, likely caused by sleeping overnight
with bad posture, apparently my pillows are too thin, I
said, o my wings give us true hearts, Höld., and the mat-
tress was all lumpy and needed to be replaced—

was I really so in love with ++++++ back then that I
stopped right in the middle of the stairway up to my
internist's office, simply stopped and stood, without
climbing up any further, while he, just having left the
internist's, appeared on the uppermost landing
ARCHANGEL like, I stopped where I stood and he climbed
slowly down and stopped when he got to me took me by
the shoulders and kissed me on the mouth

I surface early in the morning out of a mirror-slick dream,
without a clear recollection of this dream, I surface out
of a mirror-slick dream and leave behind wavy rings : 1
shock of time as we might say '1 shock of eggs'. We cannot
return to this razor-sharp element, I am reading Peter
Waterhouse and making excerpts from his work 'The
Honey Seller in the Palace Garden', he studied the
Gregorian Alphabet, which like drawings of fists and
small sea horses, I am moved, sense his pain, powerless
questions and thoughts, very many words escape me, I
find myself absorbed in a pine forest, at the foot of the
pine forest rosebuds on a sml. table (with feet like a
human's). 1 rosebud fell onto this table, floated down,
tabletop somewhat askance, I say, is going to COLLAPSE,
St Ägyd, it is profoundly sad, I say. 'Said quite clumsily,' I
read, and *was sucked up into a sitting position in the cafe
across the table from Emmy W., sitting*—in this photograph
with my hands on this sml. table which *slopes steeply* like
a deep valley, E.S. took the photo and was sucked up into
Emmy W.'s chat, recorded by E.S., and later, I say, on
another day, with other friends, the conversation centred

on demonstrations of the newest *i-phones*, to each other /
in turn, *i-phones* onto which these rose-coloured rosebuds
had drifted down onto this ltl. table BOWED DOWN under
stacks of paper and SHOUTING OUT FOR JOY, etc.

And so I woke up and immediately gave up my plans,
intentions, appointments which had occurred to me as I
surfaced, my hair *peaking* into my right eye, I say, the
snow-covered *peak* of Mt Fuji approaching me—then off
the circled portrait ran 1 strand of blood from Ely's chin
down to the floor

there were *half threads* on this (ottoman), Ely's eyes were
tear-stained in the photo, it was astonishing but on the
day of Leo N.'s burial we approached Leo N.'s daughter but
all she did was smile and laugh and I was frightened. Then
when I reached for her hand and whispered a few words I
found myself smiling and laughing and was embarrassed,
the white horror of Monteverdi Moonlight, the excrement
nagged stuck and dropped—and as it fell I found myself
laughing as if this were some kind of anecdote, I was
mesmerized, 'would you like to have my feathers' (as per
Jean Genet)

1 farewell = 1 fare well as I with the hunched back said to
E.S. it won't last much longer in any case—tiny Bishop in
baptismal font, I say, with bishop's mitre, powerful dark
tulip, full-bodied and bud which seems closely related to
bestiarium : snout of tapir in my dreams I saw the time of

day (and Utopians) the time of day was not actually the real
time (and speechless) in the early morning sudden cravings,
I say to Ely. Who had told me about bats that try to build
nests in a woman's hair in a glimmering early evening and I
trembled at the silent fluttering on my dark balcony in my
summer house in I. that 1 of these bats might be trapped
in my thinning head of hair, I say, to build a nest there
and I would have to have my head shaved to get rid of
the beast, etc., I don't actually recall a similar occurrence
during my childhood in D., there was no fluttering of bat
wings in the local farmyard, that was the time I started
reading Peter Waterhouse's new book and I took notes,
the book was astounding I *sensed* it and I wrote a letter to
the poet admiring his work, for a short time I might likely
have stopped reading Derrida and Genet exclusively and
deserted the 2 of them for Waterhouse, Ponge and
Barthes, I mean I left Derrida and Genet for a short time
and turned to other poets especially Waterhouse, it was
likely something unthinkable, the thinker (Ely) in front
of the fireplace, etc., I said to Ely, 'the Shedding of the
Body', you see

matted in my dreams, shortly before waking up in the
early morning I dreamt of a meadow daubed with daisies
and I dreamt about 1 figure in a monk's robe with the
hood drawn down over his face and 1 head of cabbage
drawn as well, it reminded me of a painting by Dalí or
Magritte, the evening before I had listened to a radio
broadcast by Margarete Mitscherlich, the voice of an old
woman, she swallowed certain sounds, I listened closely
even though I couldn't understand everything, etc.

And I could sit shedding tears for hours in the car with Ely
sitting and talking or was it E.S. that my own time was
coming soon, it made Ely / E.S. angry, not wanting to hear
my prophecy, not wanting to know the truth of my
prophecy—and I had also become very SLOW seeming to
want nothing but to laze around laze around in contemplation observing closely contemplative : as a yng. deer
e.g. might suddenly freeze in place in Pötzleindorf Park
the way it froze in place and displayed its white breast
and then the shot .. and the envelope stamped GUGGING
seeming to cast a spell setting off a string of associations,
beginning with Leo N. and the cigarettes he always gave
his patients and including the way we avoided looking into
each other's eyes : even though we were sitting next to
each other, you see, our gazes wandering, we avoided
looking into each other's eyes, seeking a *love object*, that is
what happened, isn't it, I said to E.S., Ely and searched the
corridors, in which patients came and went, or simply
lolled about, or head in arms slept deeply, dead to the
world, or I might have been looking for ++++++++ this my
Janus head was apparently searching (in vain) for
++++++++, who never came.

'These parklanders' Peter Waterhouse writes but while
reading 'most subserviently proportion' and 'estrada'
occur to me—

and on Ely's eyelashes *the weight of the world*, I thought

the swarm flooding my way : floating underneath the
swirling leaves or in the snow castle in the inner city

onrushing extended family (underneath the deep sigh of dawn's red glow on an early winter day) was basically 1 snapshot from the early 50s who was Elly Niebuhr, in the entryway lying on a carton of books it continues to arouse my heart and soul every day—yes I mean the stone lion, in front of 'Ulrich's Pub' and the sml. swarm or horde and out of those mouths the steaming breath as we depart, I say

apparently cuckoo's work. 'La Passione', Haydn : never liked it, but it might make a good title for a book, I say, am deflated defeated. Elke Erb on the phone, so *panty liners*, I say, and Elke Erb says, we're not all that angelic at least not yet, and then we go around saying to ourselves, 'today is my birthday' (like a child) and Muzette or Mama, I mean I sing with Muzette or Mama the song 'red red moth come oh come to me but I will shut the door on your little brother' .. And then I wait a few months for the lilacs, until the lilacs bloom again until the lilacs are fragrant again, and Elke Erb says, it is the sml. blossoms that are fragrant (the small crosses), not the umbels, no it is the tiny lilac blossoms that bloom and are so fragrant and we approach them and *ruffle their blossoms*, we ruffle their blossoms with the tips of our fingers, and back at home we sigh, 'please 1 more time lilacs and 1 *more time* and the tiny lilac blossoms, the tiny crosses, and once more *and then never again*', and they look like blossoms of forget-me-nots but blossoms of forget-me-nots are not fragrant and look like Muzette's eyes or Mama's. And J.D. writes and says, 'it is my name day, he doesn't say 'it's my birthday' no, he says 'it's my name day' something is getting lost, some piece of dinnerware, *some kind of headgear*, I say, and how the kitchen is swaying, the linoleum floor is confessing, I say, I am licking up the raspberry marmalade, *everything from soap opera to political correctness*, I say, was the brightness in this photo caused by the blazing glow of the winter sun or was it the reflection of the snow, I say JAGUAR I say JARGON, yes the language of flowers, I say, Muzette or Mama understood the language of flowers and it answered their questions, fulfilled their wishes : asparagus at the window, between the window panes the pelargonium, bouquets of violets, indoor linden trees in pots, I mean wondrously dear things, and dark splotches of pine, I say, '1 of the effects of running,' I say, we, Ely and I in Wertheimstein Park ran among the trees our arms outstretched and the leaves fell from the branches onto our breasts, a swirl of leaves in a cloudy sky, you see, I say the inside of my upper lip GASHED from 1 MILK TOOTH, the *unwell* voice of Margarete Mitscherlich, would like to glimmer away like this into ponds and valleys, into bells and my audience, E.S. says, only 1 vowel or aviary, E.S. says, with you the forests the bushes the large fig leaves draw together, to cool your brow, the lavender fields flocks of birds, the bats in twilight on my balcony, silently building their nests in your hair, E.S. says

dark splotches of pine wherever our Weimaraner strays, you can see that his flanks are fluttering in the wind, I say, in front of the window the rook climbs up into the winds into the breaking light. Everything composed in loneliness today ½ past 4 in the morning, this composition *that has*

enchanted me so the honey spoon got stuck in my throat :
entire swarms of bees I'm strangling—the entire world
spread with covered with poplar = MALLOW we might even
say decorated, the way blossoms bowed in the front yard
during my stay in D., I say, as tall as I am or maybe a
little shorter, they loved me and I loved them, they were
perhaps odalisques, perhaps cuckoo's weed, and I was
saddened, I was saddened, doomed etc.

What my doctor is thinking : 'we check on the patient's
foot (wrapped in black netting) bedded down in my lap,
examine it and see it's dropsy, we cover it with a heater,
even though. With bread crumbs scattered .. '

My neck my boa, one of the PEERS in the gang is painting a
triangle on the wall with the letter B in the middle of the
triangle (Boa or Bora) I feel depraved destroyed and
despondent, listening to the Bach Cantata 'Geist und
Seele sind verwirret' ('Spirit and soul become confused'),
I got carried away I ran all through the place up against
the door threw things all over the flat I pushed furniture
out of my path I grew more and more upset finally I
started to demolish my flat

and then my bath robe began to fall off I mean my bath
robe began to fall off and slid to the floor

it isn't true that I intentionally make bad choices, I mean I
choose an object I don't really want, I hold it my hand but
I don't really put it to use, I wanted another object but
because of an impulse not quite clear to me I chose the

wrong object and this was *provocative*, I say, I had very likely talked myself into believing the choice wasn't significant, 1 piece of clothing e.g. 1 piece of China 1 sandal : but I don't need 1 more sandal, I don't need 1 more piece of China I don't need any new clothes I don't need a bedside rug I don't need any holiday reading, etc., and all this piled tower high or mourning deep, I say, 1 dust vignette on my forehead, but Svetlana Geier died. 'I hear my own voice, from a distance, saying all of this, what I am writing, screaming,' J.D., 1 linen case into which the FLAME is dipped before it is swallowed 1 swallows the FLAME in order to reproduce it as poesy : in order to spit it up

the passage of burrowing through, 'this dreamfulness of my dearest mother' as per Jean Genet, this my blackthorn bush, I always fluttered somewhere near the front this was my puberty, the waiter's boots banging loudly in my favourite cafe, etc., *and I fell on my face on my favourite*, the make-up lay in a small roll—

my work ethic is 'broken harmony', escapism, scribbled down on palm leaves, I close my mouth to illumination the way he once held my mouth closed so that no one would hear my screams, and I say to my *doctor* : 'if you know what it's like in the early morning and *this sleep is so sweet*, and you'll be urinating in 10-minute intervals, and you'll find yourself regretting that you can't pee on your pillows, etc.'

MONSOON ATTACHES TO MOUNTAIN CLIMBER or : Muzette or Mama are bowling for their life, tongue is sticking to false

gums, as a bust = blossom turns in every direction and I
see my doctor's reception room with the clothes stand and
its many arms I mean, my entire attention is drawn to :
fright (fruit) feelings—and why am I at my doctor's
office—are concentrated on this clothes stand and its
parts its horrible grasping octopus arms made of dark
brown wood, and which as soon as you apply stress on any
given side, HANG, etc. anything on it a coat a scarf a back-
pack it begins to sway in such a way that you feel the need
to remove yourself from its spell.

'flamme' Fr. pennant, 'pavilion' Fr. flag, before the fem.
vagina and other gaping body parts are sewn back
together again we amuse ourselves in the 'pavilion' in a
flag language ('I can't sew,' J.D.)

and I had *spit* on it I mean I had spit on everything imag-
inable even on my own crazy phrasemakingness, I say to
Ely, in my zeal I spit on the planks of the parquet floor, on
the dirty tiles in the WC in order to *clean* them, I mean my
life is a spitting 1, I sink into indiscretion I fall victim to
the indiscrete, I say, my fate. I enter e.g. this absolute cafe,
throw my umbrella into the plastic basket at the entrance
and make my way to a sml. table in 1 far corner of the
room, and the words (wolves) claw at each other (thanks
to the language and the soap of style, etc.)

in the morning in front of the window the rook climbs up
into the winds, as Max Ernst has painted in such a stun-
ningly beautiful way, this Liszt this ivy these bandages
this melody winds : is *enslaving* itself high up into the
columns around the tree, and then I had *such a flash*

Creativity paired with an out-of-body state, so E.S.,
there in the niche near the pavement there at the edge
of the street where 'Pfaffstätten' flower-shop flowers and
bouquets collect : the 1st winter roses come into bloom,
flowers *of this sort* bloom and around the corner the
fragrance of elevated heights, I say to Ely, as I started to
climb the stairway to the loges in the Burgtheater and
felt your presence, you following my steps, you made me
dizzy, and you, hours later kissed me goodbye, I say,
time stood still I mean for 1 kiss long time began to
blossom, you see.

The week is missing 1 day, this sweet hand is missing 1
finger, the year is missing 1 moon, it has flowered my
sweet room full waking me up, it blossomed my whole
room waking me u—

then it was Monday in Berlin and so wondrous, I say, like
cotton batting. *I am celebrating High Mass*, writing is my
High Mass, *scrivere! scrivere!* As an Italian poet repeated in
her reading, my writing is my High Mass, I say, it is going
to be the end of me but I cannot stop, it causes my heart
to flutter and ache and sets my blood rushing, etc. After
the painters had finished painting the entry white, E.S.
says, she pushed a paint roller into his open mouth, still
almost a child and he was so shy, his mouth was wide open
and she shoved a paint roller into his open mouth, some
circus that was, you see. Locks and curls (lying down)
room lights dimmed (ceiling lights) I say to EvS '*am no
longer body* there is nothing of my body left am nothing
but a bag full of thorns ..'

Letter to Bernadette H. ½ past 4 in the early morning, thanking her for her most recent lines of Haiku the ones that are so difficult to make out, yet so cheerful / so contemplative, would like to invite you to meet me in the Museum Café—recently renovated : so heavenly, rook clawing his way up into the airs, magical light ..'

there was 1 small slightly deformed apple tree in Rohrmoos, on the way into the valley, did not appear to be bearing any fruit, I say, but then it did produce 2 or 3 tiny pale apples and no 1 could or would want to take the fruit away, pick the fruit, the sight so heart-rending, I wouldn't actually have been able to find the tree, its black branches twisted, gnarled, without life energy like sickly buds which had aged in virginity, they were stunted, had been unable to blossom, and there are HUMAN BUDS too who had never been able bloom, and I fell on my love my face, and then something began to glimmer in me and I will have to work something special through : *something loving*, sweet cooing doves, I say, were pecking at my bare feet. I remember the few children's books fairy tales I had when I was a child they were printed in large letters, *they were complete fairy tales*, and I as a child slowly spelling them out was able to read them with ease (later I wanted to *tear out* all of J.D.'s pages, where the greatest of craving mysteries were to be found, simply tear them out—the way one wants to harm what is loved) it began at 4 o'clock in the morning with ALPINUM, Rosa Pock and the red folding 'blinkers' on my father's 30s Talbot and ended with a ringing in my ears,

pricking in my ears, cravings, a post mortem on my own
body in the late afternoon, the 'blinker' on my father's car
was my mysterium when I was 6, the red tongue stuck out
indicated the intention to turn, etc. I no longer know
which seaside city it was I mean I can see it in my mind
but the name of the city has set, set in a sea of jetties I see
the candelabra on the shore, I stumble along the shore on
a very early morning the night was still being lit by street
lights and the light from lighthouses was still raging
swarming over the waves of the sea, the shore being
washed by the mighty waves of the sea I grab onto a light
post in order to keep from being swallowed by the sea I
remember it clearly but the name of the city has been
swallowed up—the sun set (*se couche*) it is sleeping on
pillows of clouds, I say, I wonder why E.S. loves sunflowers
so passionately while I find them a ltl. too garish. ('Ely, he,
teased me or whispering from gardens .. ') and seemed
always to be in some sort of embarrassed state, not unlike
the engl. meaning of 'self-conscious', the excrement
looked like an alligator, I say, 1 orange-coloured bouquet
of glycinias in a vase in Café Museum, but I didn't know
whether or not I had dreamt this, I was still *half-asleep*
my forearm falling down over my drunken aching ear
guillotining it and I screamed 'fleurs fleurs', like the little
dog tied up at the door to the supermarket and whining
I mean the bouquet of butterflies at the door, very
crouching, 1 ALPINUM, I say, 1 glimmering science, my
lung doctor said, it was ice cold in his examination room
and I began to shiver, and as far as my white linen jacket is
concerned, I had left it hanging over the back of a chair in

a cafe in Josefstädter Street before leaving for my appointment with the lung doctor, I couldn't stop thinking about
my linen jacket all through my appointment with my lung
doctor you see I found it difficult to pay attention to what
my lung doctor was saying because I couldn't stop thinking
about my linen jacket, the white linen jacket was so present, it simply phosphoresced, it floated through the room
and over the doctor's head, etc., the white linen jacket
emerged swaying in front of my eyes, you see, I longed for
my white linen jacket all the more so as it was palpably cold
in my lung doctor's office, I mean it was as if I were sitting
in a deep cellar and I saw my breath merging with the
image of my white linen jacket, and it seemed to me as
though I would never find my linen jacket again, and so
finally I screamed, the last crumbs of my life's days

what will I read next once I have finished reading GLAS
(by J.D.), I say to Ely, this one reading, I say, will I begin
reading GLAS from the beginning again—now that an
abyss between my outer world and my inner world has
been torn open, and I play theatre every time I so much as
dare to take a step outside my building, what Anja Utler
writes, I say to Ely, as if by Sappho, I grab *British colours*
and cover them in the *lightning-like scribbles* of my
overnight visions, I need a pair of boots and might buy
them at Marchfeld's = Mariahilfer Street, I say, I remember muff or wolf quite clearly and the wintery breath
blowing through cracks in my windows, I run off hands
folded and crouch in the bushes, etc. For some time at

receptions, I say, like the 1 where I 1st met G.K. I never ate appetizers so as to avoid carrying on a conversation with a full mouth, I could see my puffy face threatening to simply explode, I imagined my ugly face and my cheeks stuffed full making me all the more repulsive that was the beginning of our friendship, I transposed a well-starched collar lying in bed and slightly drowsy and I covered my eyes with the collar tips in order to protect them, they would otherwise have been drilled straight through by the piercing light of the ceiling lamps, I buried myself in the bolster / in the cushion I mean in the bushes full of red buds—thoroughly tender red rose buds in the bushes and I caught myself smiling while slumbering I may have imagined slumbering, I closed my eyes so tightly that they hurt, 1 closure of the lids, I say, *1 God be praised* : the way the wolves start howling at night during the winter and unexposed I yawned I flung my mouth wide open. Ely laughed and threw his head back and I could see his phar- ynx, he was like a predatory animal laughing and tipping his head back, I could see his pharynx I could see deep into HIS SOUL, I said, I see deep inside you I see deep inside your soul, I remember my words and he laughed at me and threw his head back, *'here out of a musician's tassel'*, etc.

it was a Wednesday—I am certain it was a Wednesday, in the 1st half of the night I read Peter Waterhouse's new book and that is why I had such beautiful dreams in the 2nd half of the night, I mean I dreamt that I had forgotten my white somewhat dusty wool mittens at the Literature Society and the Director of the Literature Society had sent my white somewhat dusty wool mittens back to me in an

envelope and there was a long comb in the same envelope
the comb was bent in the middle as if someone had made
an unsuccessful attempt to break it apart in the middle,
my dream was a very *good* and virtuous 1 as is the book by
Peter Waterhouse good and virtuous and *so I tramped
about in my Alpinum ('oh Eternity you Thunderous Word .. ')*

1 ennobled dwarf my coarse face, Eleonore F. sends me a
Joan Miró art card with the title 'the wing of the lark cir-
cumscribed in gold blue will return to the heart of the
corn poppy sleeping on the diamond-studded meadow'—
dark drops of pine, I am shocked. I must sink *our dirty
laundry* somewhere underground, I say to Ely ...... the way
she, E.S., bends down over me when she kisses me as if
she were kissing a sml. child and I allow it to happen (the
1st cherries the 1st snow—the years rush past so quickly
now) 'my dreams of my beloved mother now,' as per Jean
Genet, a bouquet of blackthorn, 'Kiki's Lips', Man Ray,
1929/1959, sleep deprivation, E.S. says, swollen face
caused by sleep deprivation, your face gives you away, the
light-flooded alleys in the old city have turned into a
swarm-filled alley, the flock stumbles over the snowy
cobblestone, we write 'poets' poetry'?, I say to Ely, as far
as the snow or sun photo of Elly Niebuhr is concerned, it
has flooded over the flock, I mean over the stone lions,
over the 'Ulrich Stüberl', and the white 30s bolsters in the
windows (out in plain sight, etc.), deep blue wounds I run
off with my hands folded, crouch in the bushes we strolled
along the banks of the Seine, back then in Paris, the death

of the poet merges with the image of an enormous bridge pier, I am sullen, *just sitting around here gruesomely now*, the meadow in front of the house steeply sloped, I say to Ely, and in the summer I lay out in the steeply sloping meadow in my bathing suit and the owner of the house ogled me, back in West Berlin 70/71, sat out in front of the HERRENHAUS on the steeply sloping meadow in West Berlin, 70/71, and the owner of the house was hung up on my physical appearance, Zehlendorf 70/71, and when dew drops sparkled on the grass, you see, you could tell from both the sparkling dew drops and the meadow of sparkling tears that the world was about to come to an end, and then with my dog I raced down the banks and into the bamboo forest where I stopped leant against a tree and read the letters from Mia Williams, they arrived daily and I made excerpts from what I read. At that time in the winter months KRUMME LANKE froze solid and *dancing partners* performed a lovely gliding and soaring routine, later in the year both ice and pairs melted—everything is just fine on the surface of life, Ely says.

1 spring that doesn't want to end 1 summer that doesn't want to end, but now the winter sun in my studio, I see the shadow of my head over my bookcase, I was nesting in Ely's shadow, I had observed as much as I cared to observe, and what had I actually observed, I had seen as much of the many posters hanging on the walls of my studio as I cared to see and I felt like trading my old posters for new ones, posters that existed only in my imagination, 1 reproduction of Mimmo Paladino, or photographs *blown up*, photographs which pictured me when I was 8 years

old, or something by Gerhard Richter, one of his forest pictures e.g. the old posters, I say to Ely, I've memorized the old posters on the wall, I don't want to recite them any longer, it will make me sick, if I must keep looking at them in the morning, when I open my eyes, or I might actually be more comfortable with empty walls on which only the nightly phantasmagoric curses tramp around—

I mean the tears : the dew drops and Bach's 2nd Brandenburg Concerto and the way it glimmers in the light of the early morning and the way sparks were flickering spewing light, I mean the way Charles Péguy shook his mane while stammering a quick prayer, etc., and I pray to the saints for help, I say to Ely, like Péguy did when his son was sick with typhus. It is dominant, I say to Ely, you slid into my lap, while my DOCTOR explained this and whispering to me 'you are padded,' 1 regression, I say, I regressed to being a chubby ltl. girl (archangels spit through him, Genet).

Our drives, those rouging ones, 1 seductive red in this glass, 1 intoxicating red in this glass in the meadow on the sideboard shedding its petals : at first in my hair and then on my belt and on my black woven handbag which I had slung over my shoulder and I saw him in profile (G.R.) something of a Schönberg of the 21st century with long slender fingers (fingers Schiele would have painted), I mean a crazy red and I had migraines, and my view out over the oak tree, from my balcony, where I was cowering in a rattan chair in the shade

in the morning 1 squashed dry poppy in my bed with its stem broken off—I must have slept on it all night it still

had its colour and its almost imperceptible fragrance, it
had been incubated in my anus, it was the morning after
our return from Graz, we, Ely and I, were given accommo-
dation at the Schlossberg Hotel on the edge of the city
and I spent the 2 days there in the Schlossberg Hotel
viewing paintings by contemporary artists oh my salvation having caught sight of a painting by Maria Lassnig
97, on the back of the beekeeper 1 poppy leaf, I say, there
was also a quake. And I was about to rebel in the confer-
ence 'how far are we going to go?', my heart trembled, as
if it were simply going to explode, I was *simply normal* I
mean I *was normal* and I found no words for *simply normal*
…….. it was like blood it was 1 red flower it was the waves
of the Red Sea it was traces of spittle threads of blood on a
black doublet it was sunrise, like the 1s in my 1st book of
fairy tales, there 1sunrise with red veils over its visage, I
see it in front of my face it was 8 decades ago, 'the fairy
tale of Karfunkelstein', etc.

I saw it in front of my face my sleep in a light airy transparent weave : my word dreams like sweet ltl. birds in
early spring (I could breathe on them I could touch them)
but once I woke they were no longer there, she said, 1 cos-
metic bandage on the left cheek, but I said, I don't see it,
perhaps an EATING UTENSIL a KNIFE OF SORTS (lamp
black)—1 single bush, how the valleys blaze—

Letter to Ilma R., you are sitting beside me, and I am
downing sandwiches, and instead of sharing them with
you my baby cheeks laughable (repulsive), I saw your
beautiful fine ceremonious face and in the new year would

like to sit across from you in a well-heated cafe in Vienna, speaking to each other or sharing quiet, in any case I would simply like to look into your face ...... do you think you might be able to come to Vienna, a present for me, I wish you all of the wonder of this world and others, I hold you in my arms

I hold you in my arms I *shelter* you, I dream, how often did I hear the word 'courageous' in my childhood, 'she is courageous,' or she is a fairy or she is fairy like soaring or gliding over us, or we're worried about you, we haven't seen you for a very long time or 'they dragged you out of bed in a snow night, they bedded you down on a sleigh and flew with you into the glorious winter night,' but I didn't know whether this had actually taken place or was it a dream or had my father simply kept repeating it 'we lifted you out of your bed, pulled you out of your bed out of your 1st sleep, bedded you down in a sleigh and headed out into the sparkling winter night.'

It was in the middle of the war, the region around Breslau and I met RUNGE there, Runge the painter and chastised myself, we chastised ourselves and I might have been anorexic at the time, I didn't eat the strudel I was served even though I would have liked to. Runge the painter was the same, and later I loved Klimt, Chagall, I was 17, Weiler, Magritte, Dalí, de Chiroco, Kirchner, Miró, Arp, but there (then) I was utterly drunk, my racing heart, etc., 'my heart moaning at the sight of the corn fields,' Akmatova, the black shellac tray on the kitchen table, it was actually a black plate, I had spread a checkered dish towel over the kitchen table but she didn't want to eat (E.S.) was the doctor's name ANTOINE? Why this recollection of my grandmother's family physician, he said 'too late!' (ham sandwich paint roller kitchen apron movie and cafe, cancer at 49)

carefully celebrated in severe clothing, you see

WHATEVER is below like sml. workman, whatever it is somewhat smelly ...... I say to ++++++ it was as though you had been lit by silvery flames your eye had been lit, this flaming look like the magnified eye (magnified by a magnifying glass) of Goethe's—painted by Brus, in this tattooed night, you see, this night tattooed with stars, when you started smoking out in the open in front of your Old University, and someone began reciting one of my washed out poems, here, out in the open and I turned away, etc., the drawer = foliage of the safe in our hotel room painted in a flowery motif or upholstered, I started picking, this dizzy language the moment I discovered the rose hips on the marble table in the bathroom, *my ghetto cell phone my i-phone*

as for Ely's long black robe, I say, it made him look like a priest, but it was actually a large black cape made of wool and he held it at the ready with earnest eye about to wrap it around my shoulders about to envelop me, it was a woollen scarf he had knit for me himself, he wrapped it around my shoulders and kissed me on the forehead, I was moved and that kiss reminded me of a prophecy he had made several years before, he prophesied that 1 of our friends who was depressive would kill herself, and around this time she actually did. As far as the prophesy of Brigitte Schwaiger's suicide was concerned .... it was clear to me that the title of my next book would be 'études', these tears of joy at my expectations, you see

the wooden horses : wooden drawer in the safe-deposit box of the Schlossberg Hotel in Graz, etc., which was painted with flowery vines or upholstery tempting me to pick it you see, 1 tattoo of the wooden drawer of the Schlossberg Hotel's safe-deposit box in Graz, etc., *like sml. workmen*, somewhat smelly, this vertically downward-pointing odour, like sml. workmen—still a bit smelly .... night brew night stubble, and you see, I believed I recognized him from the back, as he was unstably making his way down the narrow corridor of an approaching train, but because his neck had grown so much broader I wasn't certain it was him and I called out his name, and 'is that you?' *send me a Russian thought*, he said, and I replied, I'm going to send you a Russian thought at 11 o'clock on Friday. And me like an ELF I rush through soar through the massed-together guests, *while this dizzying language,* I find the rose hips in the vase (on the sml. marble sink in my hotel room) discover and likely pick, etc.

He was a university prof., according to E.S., he was a gypsy, I liked him, I would have liked to know him better, E.S. remarked, but it didn't come to pass, the llama in the car window, through the streets of LA, by night trimming trees blossoms text, 1 book laid out open in front of me, I was only pointing things out, I embraced him, a pile of dirty laundry on the parquet floor

I had dreamt of a stagecoach driver, of an artist without ears or with wounded ears or he was pale or hairless and had put his glasses on upside down around his ear lobes :

instead of :

he had drawn 1 picture 'about this Susi' and published it in a local paper—as things happen, and (by chance) I had just met up with a friend on the train and felt the need to write to him and to meet him again. Was it a raging storm or a minor earthquake / ground squirrel at night, baskets and boxes which had been piled up in the entryway, they had broken out of their anchoring and crashed to the floor and now blocked the *way* to the WC, you see, and my way was plastered with papers and books and I was compelled to ice axe my way to the WC, it was of course the furious storm the raging outside storm plunging down the chimney (in nights as raw as this) etc.

ich habe geträumt von einem Künstler Postillon, einem
ohne Ohren, oder er war bleich, ohne Haare und
hatte die Brillenbügel verkehrt um die Ohr—
muscheln geschlungen, so:

stalt so:

er hatte 1 Bild „über 1 SUSI" gezeichnet und
in einer Tageszeitung veröffentlicht

I dreamt about a mail-coach driver, an artist without ears,
or he was pale, without hair and had simply slung his
glasses around his ear lobes, upside down like this :

instead of :

he had drawn 1 picture 'about this Susi' and published it
in the local paper

I was waiting impatiently for the Christmas Tree Market to open, our tree seller usually showed up *on Zenta Square = with wrens* about 2 weeks before the actual celebration, the pines and firs from his own nursery in N. in the city, I say to Ely, but this year no trace of him so far, and in any case I was not looking forward to his inquiries about my well-being and it would be clear to him that this past year had gone by all too hurriedly and he would say that he was so happy to see me *so well,* all these papers IN TOW apparently because of widespread arthritis, it was affecting all my joints, and my thought processes, I tell Ely, were indeed crippled, knotted, twisted. Urs Widmer came up to me to thank me for coming to tell him that I wouldn't be able to take part in his program, I would have to excuse myself = and how he smiled and his eyes lit up ('it had the appearance of Jean Genet surrendering to his passion for writing and he turned into a flower .. ' J.D.) I was the humble 1, I say, I take the adversity on, I say, I expect storms more furious, adversity, misfortune, penetrating me, I say, I knuckle under, *I crawl,* I cross the road, I hear my bones grind as the car rolls over me, I say, their (E.S.) his blond locks FALLING SOFTLY now, I thought I had heard locks instead of readings, my sense of hearing is not as sharp as it once was, I mean my senses all of them were *getting dull,* I say, such a TULIP in her shower or her water-colour, or as Georg Kierdorf-Traut writes, Kiki's Lips (by Man Ray) were covered with foreboding or a snowfall of white incisors, white snow or fountain of incisors, whose fragrance crushed me, or as we say, the lilac bush is going to my head, etc.

Me breaking into bloom but dissonant—

have something of angel's hair = empathy for dirt and darkness : when we, Ely and I wander the streets, meeting black coaches and their fiery lanterns through the tear-filled midnight ......

these lonely ears, I listen to Keith Jarrett, the colours of dew, what I write is collage it is painting, I say to Ely, all through the approaching morning I heard the coloratura of a nightingale, I believe it was in my living room between 5 and 7 a.m., and it actually was a CD by Georg Jappe and Martin Leitner which had caused me to *lose my composure*, you see, causing my blood pressure to climb— we ate lunch in the CAFETERIA and *Kalif Storch* shovelled a meal onto the plate I had reached to him but by the time I got back to my seat my food was cold, so I took my cold food back to *Kalif Storch* and asked him to warm it up in his microwave—the trumpeter swans are actually the 1s which converse about this whole thing ('*the wild lilies of the valley have started to bud in southerly winds ..* ') oh look, my *favourite flora*

had a cramp in my leg, tripped through 3 early spring forests, I say, heard 3 mountains groan, —as for the Viennese ALPINUM or Triumvirate : snow mountain Rax Semmering, may well have been whirling illustrious circle of my recollection, I mean the peak of this snow mountain of Rax I ascended in a cog railway, a 3-year-old child stretched across the expanse of her uncle's shoulders, and thus viewed the Semmering through the windows of a train, hearing the locomotive chugging along I sensed how difficult the ascent was (rumbling mountains, etc.), and how fluid the descent into the valley down into Steyr and this brought tears to my eyes the silver bells somewhat like a distant and sudden roar of the ocean breaking loose, I say to Emmy W., today I will greet you the same way I greeted you this summer in Gmund in the breakfast room of our hotel I mean with open arms : I ran up to you with open arms and today I will run towards you with open arms although this summer I was uncertain whether it was you, you might have been in Gmund this summer in the breakfast room in the hotel 1 Phantom—I opened my arms wide and ran up to you, and in the moment my opening my arms wide you simply opened your arms as well and ran up to me, and we couldn't stop talking to each other, we believed in the PHANTOMNESS of our figures had apparently had been hiding in the foliage of the bitter orange trees, I mean the dense foliage of the bitter orange trees in the garden in the gardens of a southerly land protecting us from the world, etc.

As for the golden wing of the angel on top of the portal of the Franciscan Church, the church on Franciscan Square (the sml. cafe is there as well) glittering in the sun it hurt my eyes, it is 1 single golden wing, I tell Ely, I mean the angel on top of the Franciscan only had 1 wing, or so I claimed—my memory might be deceiving me, I say, he might well have had a 2nd wing that wasn't gold and thus had faded from memory. Good heavens what had moved me to speak about 1 angel with only 1 wing, 1 single golden wing, when there are actually 2 wings adorning this angel

today woke up with 4 versions of a Haiku, dedicated to
Dr Bernadette H., Joan Miró painted a picture with the
title 'the song of the nightingale at midnight and the early
morning rain', and then 1 musical piece by John Dowland
arose and then 1 giant glowing piece of the setting sun
appeared crowned by western clouds and I closed my eyes,
Ely whispered, just look at the sun and don't cover your
face, etc., and then Kurt N.'s cure came up, he was sitting
half lying at the cafe table with his friends and had buried
his left hand in his pants pocket and Marie Louise sank
down sank down into the DEPTHS of my HEART. So pale and
silent, 1 forest of Swiss pine you see was growing out of the
inn, or growing *out of the footprints I mean a photograph* I
had seen (P.H. had given it to me) and then the dedication
emerged 'and many returns of the day .. in a forest of bitter
orange .. ' and then I was struck by how inappropriate the
Mozart broadcast was and I LEAPT UP and yelled NO NO and
then a faded drop of blood on the tiles in the bathroom
appeared to me and then the Chinese chef of this restaurant whose name is ON and he was silently working his
magic *with chef's hat and hoisin*, and

frischgefallener Schnee =
die Blüte des Winters
Sängerin „N." ist verstummt ach.
Erfroren

für Dr Bernie H,   22.12.2010

freshly fallen snow =
winter's bloom
singer 'N.' is silenced oh,
frozen

    for Dr Bernie H.   22/12/2010

then the voice of Brigitte St rose, telling us, we are locked
into feelings and then 1 more voice rose telling us, this
angel with loose (shameless) hair and then I saw '*Infantine
of Winter*' and *1 waterfall from the flat next door*' it was
actually the sound of a vacuum cleaner, etc., and next : the
leaf turned because Ely had died, and after I had freed
myself the TRICOLOUR fell from my wallet ..

poems you dedicated to me fell to my feet, as Georg
Kierdorf-Traut said, I say, wild lilies of the valley in the
garden next door, Georg Kierdorf-Traut said, already
displaying their buds, it is simply the mice discussing it,
etc., here my favourite flowers, I say, and then the Hly.
Ghost in my mouth, I was embarrassed by the image I
thought myself to be, *we surrendered to passions, the book
overflowing with flowers* the Jean Genet book—you see 1
performance

everyone in my presence dancing. The word BLOOM danced
up in front of me on a placard on the door : BLOOM in
verse : BLOOM and Ely answered the door, 1 secret word :
BLOOM, reminding me of the word bloom, blooming,
Bloomsday, James Joyce, we move in, we step into our
friends' flat, we walk out onto the balcony, she adjusts the

rattan chair for me and naturally I dive down into the
foliage of the maple tree, 1 umbrella on the balcony, I recognized the songbirds, they weren't singing any longer, it
was high summer and they had stopped singing because it
was high summer, I sunk into the crown of the maple
trees their leaves unmoving dreams of sweet Wertheim-
stein Park, BLOOM in the doorway, high summer, billowing
dreams, I sink down into August, she arrives with the
watering can, she waters the flowers the flowers on the
balcony, 'Queen of the Night'—completely still, would
like to hold onto high summer, but in the interim
Christmas morning, 5 o'clock early morning, darkness :
Transavanguardia : Mimmo Paladino, Sandra Chia ......
sml. mad dog embraces man on a park bench, etc. ('1
certain nothing, 1 certain emptiness, just 1 moment
ago liberated bells broke out in rings', J.D.)

Ely says, he is planning to take a walk *into the forest*
(= Perchtoldsdorf) with buds *on bald branches* or take a
walk in the Vienna Woods—'the rhetorical harvest of the
lilies' is how it's written, and I IMAGINE 1 midsummer
liaison on the balcony early in the morning on Christmas
Day and in tears, as fresh as forget-me-not and we'll be
sitting in the 'Margareta' again looking through the large
window at *the silent foliage*, with God's Eye gazing across
the intersection, and that evening suddenly *staggering* and
me on crutches = *staggering*, vomiting forest of flowers, I
say to Ely, 1 design for the vomited forest of flowers, 1
pattern that is, I say, the way it is applied in literature, etc.

Scratch the back of my head, agave snow covered,
commode blown over, sitting under the palm trees

leaning up against the open window again and again,
observing construction across the way, like Gloriette, I
say, aureole ecstasy section of flowers, the world is
growing more and more spiritual

1 noblesse : this unclean red bolster a row of mother-
of-pearl buttons up 1 side, you see, likely cuckoo's work
running around in a stand of ash trees, *me so desperate*, at
that time with my 7 years, at that time with the elder tree
(1 single bush, etc.) father was there with his rod, I don't
know if he fished. And my mother's whispering shadow
was there you see and the summers had milk breasts
(*1 stagged* through the place) and the wind was very
unsettled very like lily's wind and as for this note from
Albrecht (D. as in Dürer), they reminded me to contemplate my own rapidly approaching end, and me being thus
transported into wondrously mysterious realms, and of
course I asked my father where these wondrously mysterious realms might be and what their mysteries might be,
and he described them with the words '.......' —these
notes from Albrecht (D. as in Dürer) had actually been
very troubling, they had caused me to contemplate my
own end for the 1st time in ways I never had before, had
simply lived my days with little thought or reflection as
though my own days were never numbered and would
never end—*the elliptical sentences in these notes folded as
small as I might manage, sitting on the toilet.* Does the large
black bird know he will penetrate darkness on Christmas
Day? no he loves any escape into light at any time, he
embraces any escape into light and it takes on the form of

a *bird-of-paradise flower*, etc. She came to visit Ely in the hospital with the *bird-of-paradise flower* but the sight of the bird-of-paradise flower made Ely angry and troubled, the bird-of-paradise flower had an *aggressive* presence and, I say, it frightened Ely and depressed him. You see when Muzette or Mama came to the hospital with the bird-of-paradise flower, Ely winced, oh my inner disarray, I say to E.S., after my appointment with my optometrist (I was suffering stronger and stronger panic attacks) went to the telephone booth in Nußberger Street to call Ely, to fill him in on what was happening, 'hello, hello everything's OK' and I heard his *frightful ear*, he had been waiting for my call, you see, in the featherbed of a yng. bird, etc.

I never met Othmar Zechyr, but I admired 1 of his pen-and-ink drawings in Maria G.'s living room (next to the pendulum clock), it portrayed a lock of angel's hair wound around a curler, I was enchanted, a burnt matchstick with a black tip lying on the creamer on the kitchen table—

while I am writing all this down, I say, recalling this memory draped with blossoming branches when Ely swept through the blossoming avenues of the *Prater* with his brother and I swept through the avenues I mean the avenues swept up under his feet, the colour of spring's 1st violet (and night sweats in my left elbow)

this my wound. You could hear him taking a breath between announcements, the radio announcer, I had always found his voice enchanting and it brought me to tears, Michael Köppel dreamt : of the SW window of my parents' *cabinet* of the colourful bolero of a linen blind—*hissing the summer heavens* higher and higher fluttering / sweeping in the summer wind, dreamt : being taken away in an ambulance : me as dog = in the shape of a dog, whining. When I got back home, I said to Ely, it felt as though you had under-taken a very big trip, the loneliness so great, might have been Portugal, the Nile, America, but what you had actually done was to visit a friend to celebrate *your Name Day* ('it is my Name Day,' according to J.D.), *oh with wax*, on the morning of your Saint's Day I found a few pieces of incense in a box and lit them : the fragrance wafted throughout my corpus a mercerized structure, my tennis-racket case 1 orgasm, *drowsily unconscious I am* lying flat on my bathroom floor and they brought 2 folding chairs so that I would be able to keep from falling, etc., oh sealed with wax his letters were, I say to Ely, unable to tell which colour the seals were, I believe RED perhaps aristocrat? we had to break the seal in order to open the letter and this caused the letter to regurgitate a flood of blossoms : jasmine orchids rose petals gorse blossoms anemone— they burst out the letter broke open engorging its con-tents, the letter paper was pale blue, the handwriting tender difficult to make out.

Still life in the morning, both brown shoe inserts sweat through and on the floor next to my bed 1 black stocking next to that 1 pair of white panties folded tightly together. *Sulking* and the family photo framed with yarn, I say, and 1 book overflowing with flowers (Jean Genet), my soul swollen, I say, I am reading Claude Simon 'will

you take note?' = yng. woman before her 1st night of love,
I can feel the sip of water I want to take sliding down the
back of my throat and me barely escaping a choking fit—
that was the exception, most of the time I choke when
I drink water, I say, we walk past the pharmacy 'the
FURIOUSLY hly. Ghost'

(insert) :
ah with wax or a poem at the end of the year 2010, for E.S.

how beautiful the colour RED is on her breast in the forest in
the frost the approaching temperament, I recognize it, it is
turning, turning around indicating the intention : indicating
marginalization : something NEW something POMP something
cape-like RED albatross like

                       or
completely RED: flaming fluff 1 fleece with thorns
                       apparitions
needles 1 turn : time 1 turn, return perhaps, it, time
                       indicates
a stranger's another shoulder, *conceals*, I say, RED: Adonis rose,
initializing *something bud like* (RED)—in those wild bouquets
                       in
deepest heart of winter : deepest wood, flora's bloody RED
tears,
the doll

this sulking, I say, have I actually *worked my way* through all possible doctors, in my seclusion helplessness frailty, difficulty breathing overnight cried coughed or coughed my lungs out, *at a trot*, I say, I mean my body keeps me at a trot, etc., apathetic and agitated at the same time, wreath of roses my neediness, with wild violets and enthrallingly gorgeous roses on store counter, vulgarly butchered, this butchered beauty on the store counter, gorgeous butchered roses on the store counter, gilt-edged : these gilt-edged roses, heart-rending the way they howl, scream, with gorgeous blossoms open they accuse us, they accuse the knives, the scissors, the pincers, when they are cut mowed weeded in those glass-covered greenhouses, rose shears such hidden grace, you see, arms full of roses, at once Muzette and Mama like, arms overflowing with roses, and the way she stepped out of the large rose garden in D.

(*'you see her pushing the cuttings out of her way'*)

we will pull the ROSES = ROBES out from under their skirts, I mean, out on the streets we will pull bouquets of roses out from under muslin skirts, without the actual fragrance of roses arising, as we pull the bouquets of roses out from under their skirts, and I pull I pull the rose bushes out from under from under Muslim skirts how I am weeding my heart, with 1 beat of my wings, etc.

As far as the appearance of my father's handwriting in his letters goes, I say, the handwritten letters grew frailer and

frailer (strewn like wilted flowers, from line to line frailer
= more and more cursory, more and more difficult to decipher his hand at best until the end of a letter.

You see, you only see fields of gladiola, only gladiola or
bird-of-paradise flowers, day lilies, irises grew and spread
(see above : 'she came into the patient's room with bird-
of-paradise flowers, she carried the bird-of-paradise
flowers straight up in front of her as though it were a
burning candle she didn't want to extinguish .. ')—what
I mean to say is at the end of my father's letter only 'd.P.'
was legible, d.P. meaning your 'devoted Papa'

(Collection of gladiolas bird-of-paradise flowers day lilies
irises wrapped in a cloth, I mean covered), my illness = my
sputum, especially at night, at times I almost choke, *the
bells in the garden in D.*

(*'I sprout object erotic'*)

Forest path and stream in the evening late, the deer drink
water, her appetite grew before she died, you see, she ate a
handful of cherries, in the hospital, she seemed distressed
when I left her she had a combative face when I left her, 1
broken autumn leaf in her hand embroidery broken
through, the ambulance crushing stems brown flattened
brown as if painted on the floor, I mean stems without
blossoms : CORPSE I touch it 1 flower with its blossom torn
off, and the dead flower petals strewn everywhere, in the
WC the bird-of-paradise flower wilting stems tightly bent,
and then I remember *sciences* I must catch up on : too late
too late, I say. The transparent line of a poem, I say to Ely,

the places I've been with Ely, I say, Theresa 'Reinhold will inspire the buds actually the stigmata, hard to make out in bouquets on hands and feet on the edge of the forest—hedges, etc.' The thorns and the red glow of dawn, I say, I had a collection of fairy tales, I say, the red glow of dawn and red veils and hospital rooms : I was discouraged, with kimono-styled jacket

I woke up and had the *ornament of a dream* still in me wanted devastation : wanted to keep the penetration of wakefulness away, this state of wakefulness was 1 alien element wounding me I wanted repose forever in this ornament of a dream, I say, you see, the creeper = caress of a tea rose bush ....

Now, *the entire year through,* Sabine H. writes, over-listened to my Patty Smith portable CD, wolf returning from my cousins, etc.

1 up in arms, I say to Ely, this tickle in 1s throat, this protest against waking up, I say, my underarms viscous slime when the light shines in from the right the shadow of my writing hand falls on the page : a giant shadow with pointed ornamentation, it reminds me of the hidden structure of a word-cascade, I say, my *Bolero* not com-pletely rested and it gushed out of my eyes, I say to Ely, we will have to hurry, mail too slow, *we will need a fax,* you see, we will need a meaningful and serious fax, I mean, without hollowness without disruption my lg. underarms covered in perspiration because I pressed them into my

face overnight : pressed them into my face, I say, and as I awoke, I wrung them, I say to Ely he is my everything, I make a drawing of a Dalí flagon, and write beneath it 'my everything', etc.

There is still a lot of sleep in my eyes and I have no will of my own I often think of Emmy W., she is 1 fountainhead, I say to Ely, full of mystery, I say, her character is clearly on display, she is always standing on a stage, very subtle, she is always acting in my favourite cafe, I want to watch her, she amuses me, what shall I say with my little basket on my arm ('my little yellow basket,' she sings 'my little yellow basket' it was Ely's favourite, like ELLA, Ella Fitzgerald's 'my little yellow basket'), she is dancing a Bolero, I am constructing a mnemonic to help me remember, someone writes 'at heart unchanged', age has left me unchanged at heart, etc., I slip under my blanket, my lft. arm is freezing, 1 bird feather in my house slipper—

I listen to ancient music early in the morning e.g. a canaria, I see swarms of yellow birds in my studio, my studio is full of lemon-yellow birds canaries I believe, they are beautiful birds they sing they sing lemon-yellow songs on 1 thousand harps, I say, I hear his voice on the radio, Michael Köppel, over the course of the broadcast, about to initiate a sml. laugh as if someone were teasing him, the timbre of voice delights me, I can't listen to anyone else, 'I would like to meet you,' I write to Michael Köppel, Michael = like Brigitte, if I don't think Michael I think Brigitte. E.S. helps me *with my coat buttons it up,* 'you are

my doll,' she says, she dresses me, buttons up my coat, my
coat is too large for me now, have no will of my own, I am
in another world, I say, I am with the canaries, canary
birds, they are whirring around my studio, whole grapes :
are hanging on the net strung out across my studio
('queer'), the piano music is by Robert Schumann and I
have fallen in love with his voice, I am enchanted with his
voice, I say, I would like to meet him, we will sit across
from each other and look at each other, nothing more—
and then Emmy W. will walk into the room and stomp
across the dirty floor of Café Tirolerhof I believe she will
give us a Csárdás, I will watch and wait, I will wait for his
voice his voice will sound sweet to me I will be happy, I say
to Ely, Emmy W. will *dance out of* the room and leave us
alone, I will switch the radio on, he will begin speaking at
5 a.m., today a number of laughs beginning Loreley like,
something like 1 sweet trembling stumbling protest in his
voice, he spoke to me, I say, and his attempt at 1 laugh, it
wasn't really a laugh, it was the memory of a sml. sweet
laugh, the attempt at a laugh I mean the infinity of infi-
nite numbers of lemon-yellow canaries or Canary Islands
present in my studio.

I am in a phase now where I am unable to read the time, a
little TUMMY EXALTATION, in a state of delirium, etc. I am
surrounded by 1 violet, E.S. knit my white communion
scarf, with a vignette, I see *1 gloriette* in the distance I
mean I see a gloriette in the window (1 new construction
and vis-á-vis 1 snowdrift) my hands smelling of cookies,
etc.

As if looking into a mirror, I say to Ely, a few minutes before waking up I dream, that I am waking up, someone bends over me and asks me the meaning of a few Fr. words, the song of a lark of a nightingale *of a sparrow*, a rush mat in the bread box, bird feathers in my house slippers again, WOODEN LIMBS overnight, this veil of hair over my eyes, lilies of the valley, hidden lilies of the valley in a stranger's garden on the street, once in Bad Ischl, I say to Ely, *I am choking on this argot—*

1 wave 1 swipe over my closed eyes, 1 cuckoo's laugh, echo of a cuckoo's laugh in my heart, *her eyes sleep-filled*, she showed it to me in the lift, standing obliquely, with eyes closed leaning up against the back wall of the lift, she then stood up straight and opened her eyes thereby cutting off my breath, etc. I mean these lips, Kiki's Lips by Man Ray covered in snow crystals and some believe it is Kiki's incisors this white SPUTUM or SCUM, when I open my eyes I see letters *written in longhand*, ltl. finger *moans* from so much knitting, E.S. says, ponytail to the left in my dream I see myself and am ashamed of myself, I invent an artific. Fr. language in my dreams, I say, e.g. 'recoller' and look it up in my dictionnaire to see if it does exist, have an upset stomach, sit with Ely in Café Prückel at a sml. table, all too close to the next table, hear every word spoken, am unable to concentrate on my conversation with Ely, greet the bronchitis owner of the cafe, at the next table talking loudly, gesturing, 2 overweight female students, 2 overweight birds circling through the room, we're expecting Valérie B., and she appears with a BUSH FULL of anemones covering her face, she kisses me 3x the way the Swiss do

and I am already on my descent, I ask Valérie B., somewhat unsure of herself she says 'not yet', we draw away, we
pray the Rosary our end is nigh, my *family doctor* can tell
from the smell of 1s bodily excretions whether or not 1's
tumour is malignant, you see.

'My monogram is made of ivy,' Jean Genet, I choose 1 of
Ely's handkerchiefs with his monogram and hold it over
my mouth as I leave the cafe so as not to breathe in the
cold winter air—

saw a squirrel on the title page of *Animal Protection
Journal running* through the park grounds you see, ears
pointed with tufts of fur behind, it ran and ran through
my building, at the same time in front of me, I mean at
the same time it lay on a stack of books in the entryway
and my heart was pounding, this squirrel observed me
with human eyes and reminded me of my 91-year-old
language professor *Frau Röder* who lives on Castelli Street,
she tutors me in English and French once a week as I grow
more and more speechless, gusts of wind through the
bushes, *Phoebus with arms outstretched* I glow, etc. Whenever I sit on the toilet seat, staring down at Phoebus, I
mean staring down at the tiles of the WC, I saw 4 or 5
silverfish or mosquitos *flitting around*, this *creature
plumage* this bird-of-paradise flower in the corner of the
WC, was wilted, broken, broken apart, broken to bits in a
jug it had given up, I say. Had fallen asleep, I say, the art-
cards correspondence between me and Wolfgang Ernst
had fallen asleep and I regretted that—

'This picture is for you,' Barbara Alms writes from Bremen, 'I was in the Tate Museum London over Christmas where I saw a wonderful Mantegna, the infant Jesus standing there and holding a globe in one hand and an olive branch in the other, *the Virgin Mary was sewing*, John the Baptist was pointing at Jesus and Joseph was looking off to the side, 1 orange-tree orchard surrounds the Holy Family ...... 1 violet surrounds me.'

Blood on my hand faeces in my hand the folded brown air-mail letters in the WC, cooking : stirring with J.D., Jean Genet, Peter Waterhouse, kitchen apron = readings, in the garden of pleasures poesy, the park grounds of intellect presentiment and hymns of mourning—1 *leaping* paradox of this sort : as for our coincidental meeting with ...... in Schönbrunn, was it 1 *budding walk* of a special sort, you see we snaked along passage ways or labyrinths, lost our way in the ruins of bushes, stylishly trimmed hedges and branches, and came to a stop again and again, threw our arms around each other, showered each other with kisses, the maze contained all of the flowers absent in all of the bouquets, J.D., but it was actually 1 anthology : 1 flower harvest the way we wove crowns of blossoms around each other's heads—and when we woke up something was pulsing in my studio it was the rain falling on my windows (wings and 'glittering splitter', etc.), *your corpus*, I say to Ely, as for this domesticity, as for this *daywork,* it trans-formed itself into a patterned IRONING BOARD, a *Prussian sea manoeuvre*—'Papa' I screamed and ran down the stairs to meet him, 'Hans is going to take us to the countryside with him, etc.', Papa didn't answer—it was an animated dream with serious signals, heaps and piles of white Swiss Health Lozenges rise on Gebirgsstraße for my wounded throat. 10 days in the country, I imagined myself lighting up this returning with *raw* cheeks, I throw crumpled-up Kleenex across the dining table, Hans had eaten melted chocolate that had stuck to his fingers, still encased in my husk diving into my dream, I say to Ely, he will light up this day, my intestinal flora is greening, I imagined 2 olive trees lying across from each other in a forested avenue each taking 1 step back, and they bow to each other. 1 stream of longing ran all the way through my dream and I was unable to decipher its code—my indolence kept me from doffing a crown of roses = kept me from satisfying my lower body, like 1 lamb I held still, I say to Ely, as he my breasts, I say, I had curls like 1 lamb, the way 1 often does when profoundly frightened the grandfather clock chimes, rose hips on the marble table in Budapest, I say, I wed these objects, take on their shape, I recover, this dream you see has made me = healthy, something like a dark-blue children's uniform lay on the street, as though it had been thrown out of a (moving) car I mean this thing had torn loose, these were awestruck times, especially DAISIES

mostly violet happenings actually waterfalls you see they broke my neck, I say to E.S., she had sleep-filled eyes, showed it to me in the lift, red umbels red bushes in the hallway pink hydrangea and clouds in the hallway, flower-budding walks with Ely, in the middle of winter (or on a hallway chair under shimmering heavens), the hly. Ghost flew into my mouth, my chirping pose, I say to Ely, on the

sweet green avenues of slumber, it must be dark dabs of
sap on the fir tree in the front yard, THE SUN IS MANIAC

Kiki's Lips by Man Ray, *archangels spit into him*, Jean Genet,
I blow the day out, check the Fr. dictionnaire, mostly
invented, I say, I need yng. meat, Otto B. says, in Café
Museum in the 90s—just sitting around here GRUESOMELY
now, I could sit here writing all morning, no longer
counting the hours, Empedocles, by Höld.

'those lamping eyes' (solch lampende Augen), Edmund
Spenser, it snowed it snowed on Kiki's eyes, Man Ray said,
he decided to photograph only the mouth, or a giant pair
of lips soaring across the heavens, decided to paint, 1st a
picture and then gave it the title 'les amoureux', and this
was true, this is what Georg Kierdorf-Traut wrote me, he
knew this mouth and decades ago he had seen this mouth
that was my mouth, and kept it as a beautiful memory
despite the fact that I was not in concord with this appearance of my lips, because of their narrowness, I say, what
was printed onto these lips, ice crystals apparently, tender
cloud plumage, 1 sweet bouquet of dew and stars

I lie half the day covered in hand-knit wool blanket, when
I was injected in the HERA I read the Collected Works of
Sigmund Freud, and mimicked his brilliant style, found
myself tumbling into the skating rink in Bad Ischl, my eye
caught fire on the rushing floods of the Traun in its
glittering July. We traded clothes, E.S. offered me her
autumn coat, and I offer her my red bolero, we're behaving
like ltl. girls, rushing through foliage and ivy, *we are Utopians*.

Tear-filled rejection (sooty) this rat imitation in the bread
department of the local supermarket, it frightened me :
jagged mouths and jagged tails, ascetic river banks,
boundlessly feverish red sunset brushed full of cortisol,
whooshing into the beyond, everything composed out of
loneliness, today 4.30 a.m., this precise exact brain early
in the morning, this holy brain that knows everything, I
say to Ely, this by your endless conversation between you
and me, I say, everything swirled around in my head I saw
myself as everyone, I was disabled—'overnight thinking of
Germany ..' (Heine) and I see Friedrich Hölderlin, as if
there were 1 swallow in my breast : smoking swallow—
salon, 'don't you think we should TAKE A TRIP together' I
ask E.S., with our bosom-buddy archangel co-op sweater,
I grimace in front of the mirror. 'dearest Elisabeth I won't
be able to attend your reading in the ALTEN SCHMIEDE
(Old Blacksmith Shop) it makes me sad, I had wanted to
down to swallow 𝄢 the piano rolls (Egon Schiele) coming
out of your mouth, but my time is crumbling to pieces I
love your thinking eye and face, am just sitting around
here GRUESOMELY now ..' you are being addressed by your
name now, I say to Ely, but I don't actually mean you, I say
to Ely, I pass by the yew trees in the Votive Park, bluebell
trees by the trunks of the oak trees and Swiss pine, it was
summer and I believe it was a woman approaching me
asking me for an autograph, etc. *the reception on the other
side of the Votive Park was mine*, I say, 1 marble stele perhaps, I say, 1 figure whose arms had been elongated into a
harmonica-like instrument, you were named but I didn't
mean you, I say to Ely, the panic of swirling leaves, it was
late summer early autumn someone was approaching me

asking for an autograph with a piece of paper in her hand
her hand might have been trembling—while she reached
over to me: this person was a woman I believe, young, I
looked for a pen in my shoulder bag, the trees in Votive
Park had begun to flutter in the autumn winds, I say, the
arms of my stele had been elongated into a harmonica-like
instrument, you were named, I say to Ely, but I didn't
mean you, it was this way throughout the writing of
this book, the people named in this book are not actually
those people, I say, until sometime after midnight I page
through Man Ray's works

I hadn't received any mail the previous day, and now I'm
afraid, I'll have to wait through another day without any
mail delivery. I mean there will be days without any con-
tact with the wide world, and I would be completely cut off
from the rest of the world, the wide world had grown
silent or perhaps I had suddenly been struck dumb.
Brigitte F. in jeans on the podium bowing low from the
middle of her body, she seems to have chosen this pose.

I revived *those feelings*, I was able to view them in all their
profound closeness and all their profound intimacy, you
see, while sensing this intimacy, while *zeroing in on it*, I
forgot to breathe I was so overcome, here I was dealing
with nudity, with open wounds profoundly painful : 1
horde of butterflies 1 pack of wolves : my feelings from
that time lay stunned like an open wound, and I began to
lick my wounds—

steep slope or honey sweet, I say, it was surely 1 abstract
bodily appeal, 1 sweet lamb under blue heavens : you
often find this in Roman Catholic churches, Marcel B.

says, 'oh', I say, after a long dream, 'with long the longest steps in which he found his handkerchief, the light brown bench under the light of the morning sun in the garden'

I traced the *Phoenix*, I say, I telephoned EvS that morning, I saw a horde of butterflies, I whispered DUFY THE DANUBE, I say DUFY THE DANUBE is such a powerfully attractive force whoever wades into this river never comes out alive, I say, will simply be fished out with lungs full of water, there where we see the stone lion, recently Brigitte Schwaiger waded in and never came out.

He was in the hospital garden this spring (because the 1st buds), I say, she read Gogol's Coat to him and he felt protected, then the ice-cream cone and sml. Beer, etc., as the magnolias began to shoot up, the Day Moon appeared over the hedges, I knew the lilacs would soon begin to blossom, the child would soon be baptized under the New Moon, I say, *the baggage of my memory*—Man Ray's pearl-like portraits of women (*Tears*), flowing locks white at the end, she said, tulip kisses, 1 sweet bouquet of dew and stars on her left cheek, I say, and we fled to the edge of the forest where we found patterns and shadows of the DARK ROSE (in Man Ray's *Portraits of Women*) I mean of kisses of tasting of licking of cultured dust (Man Ray)

was asked if I were cold were frozen were pared down as if Vlado had just appeared on the balcony as if E.S. were applauding as we made our way to the exit of Wertheim-stein Park, you see Hildegard von Bingen *wore a crown on*

her head, she pulled my sweater tight and I was her doll—
it snowed it snowed on Kiki's lips, according to Man Ray
...... onto the balcony as I walked out with bare feet in the
morning *the knotgrass* the gnarled branches at the railing
as if in late winter breasts : buds on branches opening, oh
the branch lay there as if it had entrusted itself to me with
knowing shafts of light—1 limb broken off and the night
wind (blew) it onto my breast, etc.

is seeking is seeking to plant a kiss on the grapes, Ely says, it
was in a dream, I say, he was wearing a bright blue hand-
knit sweater and handed E.S. a white tulip while gazing
deeply into her eyes, overnight cramps in my leg and I
screamed—my dance muscles my breviary, I had slept 9
hours and I haven't written to Heinz Schafroth for some
time, he seemed so distant, I searched for him but in his
feelings, she had tiny bird feathers on her thin fingers,
she held onto a gnarled branch, deeply fearful she held
tight. I believe I no longer wanted to stand up, I say to Ely,
I no longer wanted to cut myself off from this state of
glimmering or dreaming, someone will have to bring me
my breakfast on a tray, to my bedside, but I didn't want
to say a thing (doing incessantly disciplined exercises for
the entire world, etc.)

it snowed it snowed on Kiki's Lips, 1 powdered sugar 1
frost, Man Ray's pearl-like portraits of women ('Tears'),
flowing locks white at the end, she says, the tulip kisses,
I stammered and I staggered and my eye lit up on the
rushing Traun in its July glistening. etc. and *I grew more
and more speechless*, he cut off 1 end of his scarf, in Café

Rathaus, he didn't want to say why, 'your sweet white paw out the back seat of your car resting on my shoulder,' I say to Ulla B., she reached from the back seat of her car and lay her sweet white paw on my shoulder, her eyes in sml. brooks

the poster portraying me, sitting on a stool, on the door to my bedroom, and Ely said, now you'll see the 2 of us embracing, then 1 poster portraying me, sitting on a barstool, hung in Fritsch's bookstore and seeing it I smiled remembering it you see, this was once my life, etc., we searched for and found works by ETA Hoffman which stood at the door welcoming us—the alders wolves and foxes swayed from side to side in my living-room window and 1 fiery roar could be heard and I trembled. I opened my arms, received their blessing, you see, the alders wolves and foxes opened their arms and embraced us and I run with my deep blue wounds and folded hands, me crouching down in the underbrush

'I avoided learning to sew,' J.D. says, my eye my ocular feelings tore open in the 1st hours of morning, I was driven out of my dream, I say to Ely, there was no return but I longed for the sweetness of dreaming, we *forested the building of a bridge* I didn't like me preferring underbrush (am bird fluttering am realm of thorns)—

this recollection of a newspaper photo of a death's-head monkey zoologist T.N. was studying, monkey on his shoulder, monkey *pinching* zoologist's ear lobe or

whispering something to him was apparently led to 1
of my morning dreams in which I hand in hand with a
monkey-human, driving to an animal shelter in a taxi in
order to get this monkey-human off my hands : my aversion to monkey-humans powerful, my own housing too
limited for this kind of sheltering, etc. In winter 1 swipe
across my closed eyes 1 cuckoo's scream, echo of 1cuckoo's
scream in my heart, *this argot stuck in my maw*, my language movements break free, *my make-up* lay in small
rolls at the entrance to my grandparents' delicatessen,
my grandmother put the ham wraps into my mouth, I
break down into indiscretion, I fall victim to indiscretion,
I enter the absolute pub, THROW my umbrella into the
brass basket and make my way to the sml. table in the
corner of the pub, the words (= wolves) claw each other
fall for each other, were we clawed into each other had we
simply fallen under each other's magic spell, etc., *my fear
that I am falling on my sword* 'and my words fail me' J.D.

to the sewing machine with my black shoulder bag, I say, I
have seen snow-covered mountains, and perhaps a bird
soaring high into the heavens (on television) the fir trees
on the edge of the forest 1 gigantic deference, Teutons
presumably (look it up!), camels (hunt) through the icy
heavens, etc., you will find the word AMNESTY on a piece of
paper, the unremarkable things of life next to all of life's
grandness, I say, yellow roses tea roses I mean, *me shred-
ded*, I say, can you tell me why, I write to Siegfried Höllrigl,
I start crying when I read your letters, 1 glory or gloire

Christ crucified, when the blackthorn in his eyes glanced at me you see, *and he was crying up above his belt*, how wondrous oh! : me drunk on music, in the early morning, I mean everything must now be echoed in J.D.'s death bells—Kiki's Lips (as per Man Ray) were covered with a presentiment or snowfall of white incisors : 1 white snow or fountain of powdered sugar whose scent crushed me, or as 1 says, the lilacs are going to my head, etc., I woke up with locks 'Isar cabin', my eyelashes stuck together = fig tree leaves at the entrance to the outdoor cafe and stroked my forehead, I might have been the Alpha Creature. Did *you* explain it to me *tenderly*, I say too Ely, 1s hair turns white before 1 dies, in my dreams my hands were incense, Andreas O.'s hair turned white BEFORE HE RETURNED HOME, but he was unable to stand up from his chair when he celebrated his birthday with his friends—bodies performance, my throat will be illuminated, I woke up in the gap of early morning between the curtains 1 soaring heaven like 1s in the paintings of the old masters, 1 trembling flashlight, I am speaking with Brigitte St, and sometime around midnight, I wake up in my bed fully clothed and lie for a long while on my right ear, etc.

Toned Lips = Kiki's Lips ?, I misheard it, I had heard 'toned lips' and I still lay there with my eyes closed or with my eyes wide open and look look, I do not speak only look observe watch the world, with 'toned lips' and eyes, me on the verge of crying in the early morning and as I wake up to Liszt's variation 'tenderly my songs implore' taken from Franz Schubert's *Swan Song*, etc. It's about *siskins* about a 'single siskin' (I have a sketch I made of a 'single siskin'

and it is lying in front of Muzette's door or Mama's his
song in wordless tones, you see, before the siskin enters
Muzette's or Mama's dwelling, and hours later the siskin
in front of Sister Roswitha's door his song in dark tones,
so before the siskin enters Sister Roswitha's dwelling his
winged voice, and so

the siskin enters, in Muzette's or Mama's dwelling with a
last scream of pain and crying while the *recorder* senses
that his text has been erased is faded ruined, and basically
everything completed is due, aching, mis-formed, I say)
then when I was in great pain, I say, he, Ely took me in his
arms, cradled me in his arms like a crying baby—

my barriers my birch grove or my wet snowshoes on
Jean Genet's *The Diary of a Thief*, and I went to meet my
auntie at the tube station and she was already waiting for
me at the station and we went from the station to her
place and I was embraced by her hospitality, 1 roasted
chicken 1 coffee 1 opium cake as dessert, but all I see is
her smiling mouth liberated from her face.

And under these pale heavens the bushes in the forest
everything in green 1 gap 1 confession 5 o'clock in the
early morning, so kissing the brown fields the orange
heavens where have I seen these twisted forests before, in

which paintings the shafts of light of this presentiment, I grasp them, smelling their life-scent, I say, their twigs and crowns, I lie on my back the morning blue and white heaven's gap in my notebook 1 tiny dead insect, various good fortune and every morning, the light brown bench in the garden ...... my brain cycles through much bony matter, here to visit me in sunlight, etc., in an armchair in the entryway under the flickering heavens, upholstery meadow-like on my cheek, I say, viscous like syrup the movement of my thoughts, and she took her handkerchief out *to wipe my tears away*

1 violet embraces me rumbling in my breast etc. 1 single hand-warmer (knit by Marie Luise) *claws in my notebook* my pain my laziness my grim laziness, I say, 1 yng. and graceful deer in my dream so homeless in the night, standing in front of my window over the course of the day roaming through the countryside by night everything blurred nowhere comforting, so homeless by night, I say to Ely when screaming pain wrenches itself away from me, in Petrarch's work I read 'my tender transalpine loneliness' and 'the beginning does not appear to be sad enough', it weighs on my heart, the blond mimosa buds at the exit already wilting. In hedges on altars across avenues. Mimosa trees across avenues on altars, between shampoos and pedicures immerse ourselves in a few pages of Genet's *The Diary of a Thief*, making excerpts, etc., slept wrapped up in my own hair, at this time who was my lover, I ask

myself ('to me *shall I give you beauty*?'), as though we had
broken through broken a long-term relationship, sullied
it, COMPLETELY soiled both hands with faeces, in Warsaw
fortune-tellers then prophesying as for what was whispered then in the 80s, this scene played out in a stand
of olive trees not far from the Capital City actually in
an olive grove, etc., where I was promised a long life and
great loneliness, I took my hand out of hers and the next
morning gave no further thought to her prophecy

dull, you see, her entire group was dull, I say, you open a
number of zones of the spirit to me, I say to Ely, even
more and tear-filled. Eleonore F. is sending me 'the song of
the nightingale around midnight and the morning rain'—
the sml. black pennant or eyelashes on my left eye darken
my view, there were umbels and ravens and numbers of
animals hunting each other, I say to Ely and I was able to
run again and spin and hop too and we embraced each
other after a long time apart and I kissed you tenderly and
sought the inside of your sweet mouth. As far as the rose-
red cover of my notebook is concerned, I say, rose-red
binder over my notebook, claws in my notebook, I say,
rose-red cover like the binder I had as a schoolchild, Big
Ben on the cover of my notebook, Ely says, I darkened
Phoebus, 1 pack of rose-red hairpins in the hallway, he
pulled my vest tight *I was his doll*, how long will the sun
keep rising for us, Ely asks, I am awakening but have
become dissonant, etc.

The hyacinths : why 2 sml. stones in the flower pot and next to that *1 sweet stand of underbrush*, and a moss cape like a light green fur collar ......

he was in his travelling clothes in a flowery mass of blossoms (claws of my notebook seeded with Parma violets), 1 green plastic basket on stilts, I say to Ely, scent of a hyacinth in my dwelling, strands of hair stuck to my left eye, with hands folded through the household benediction—I give the newspaper boy a few coins without taking the paper ('AUGUSTIN') ...... here, the dots, as they are in my head, I say, 1 pain-stitch, after a 1-year stay in Rome, Villa Massimo, and Marcel B. returned to Dresden, Dresden therapy- or tulip-cheeks transparent like X-Rays, my body filled with air, empty aluminium packets (Aspirin) dashed into quivering branches, almost falling asleep while writing a letter, I say to Ely, spent most of my time with apples, as for the *aspirating forest* in Altaussee, it is raining from the branches of the fig tree and thereby making breathing easier, it smelled of the foods of the soul and salt and we held hands and looked into each other's eyes

so dream-filled the countryside : opened dreamt Robinia countryside recollected, feathered, the heavens soaring, dampened winds, gentle winds in D. I mean on the cracked and sloping fences, she screamed : 'daisies' she screamed, 'pale transparent tulips LIKE X-RAYS,' she screamed, 'such phenomena' and me like *a Gecko* sticking to the walls of this room / benches, and me in my rigidity, etc.

In these 'writings', how should we translate this perhaps 'what has been written', 'written things' that 'which is drawn out beyond these lines' ...... I mean the spattering rain, the blotched mountains, the jagged petals the deep-sea bouquets, we puffed and gasped up the mountain road and slugs lay on the damp planks, Elke Erb telephoned, I have a plebian voice—1 maze of furniture 1 maze of hyacinth pots—as for *Wally's* shadow, I say to E.S., did you see him 2 or 3 years after his death in the bushes and forests of Ossiach, I mean, Wally's shadow appeared to you in the bushes and forests of Ossiach I mean Wally's shadow snaked around the bushes and forests of Ossiach I mean you could see his footprint in the meadows and bushes, it appeared and disappeared, you encountered Wally's shadow on forest paths and in the mountains, it appeared on the hem of the heavens and in streams and rivers and on the invisible lake where ice birds. You reached for him but you couldn't catch him : he dissolved as soon as you grabbed for him

falling like a bird into the *frills of the forest*, I say, into the resedas, Ely's monogram in my lap, 1 embroidered 'E' in a blue flowing hand, rotting fruit, received a bouquet of mimosas from Nantes, from Aurélie Le Née, she lives on the street of the red chapeau, you see, the *flare up* as soon as her lover's tongue inside her ear, etc. tying blossoms and stems into sheaves or a bouquet, according to Valérie B., the tiny shako made out of folded newspaper on the tile floor of the WC I believe Ely must have made it, I read 'works of art', '1-day outings' and my heart begins to

flee it flees to memories of the time we took '1-day outings'
it must have been in an earlier life, I say, 3 resedas
between my lips, ate an apricot in February, bit into an
apricot in the fern, 1 flake melted on my lips, poet and
composer Gerhard R. can be compared to a *metronome*,
how is it that we now have circles of yng. neurotic women
who spend all of their time knitting jackets, the hens you
see flowers torn apart ...... as for adhesion or the red yarn,
I say, I automatically take on the colouring of this person /
these persons, and I immediately speak with their intona-
tion their volume or their insularity, oh with their faculty
without wanting to, I say, with hands raised, feet flying,
screaming, gesturing, I love Emmy W.'s sparkling flashing
intelligence etc.

('dear Aurélie Le Née, such a beautiful letter (with fragrant
mimosas) it made me so happy thank you dearly ...... ')

we bought a notebook for vocabulary and I am writing
special terms down in the left column, the ltl. prima
donnas on the right, my notebook's claws e.g. suddenly
at 5 in the morning scrawled across the meadow, the
appearance of 1 unopened letter it is Maria G.'s handwriting, it lay there on my bed, but then disappeared,
I say to Ely, how do you explain it, *1 of my socks*, I would
like to make you a present of all sorts of things, like band
music, Alex Wied telephoned me 'violet in my ear bedded
in moss, snow-covered agaves scattered rocking chair'
('dog in poppy forest' Ulrich Tarlatt), on Easter I rock into
the branches, I say to Ely, daisies likely, 'oh you my sweet

soul'—mood and violet-like, almost fall asleep writing a letter, I say to Ely he is my Intimus.

End of February our 2nd blossom outing still before us

2.18.2011

Supplement on 19.2.2011

I haven't moved an inch I say to Rumi or E.S., just sitting
around here gruesomely now—come to me after my death
1 more time as if I were still alive that would do me endless good. I will experience the perceptible in the after-
world more profoundly as though you were still holding
my hand, and with my rotting eyes I will splash around *on
the back of the lake* looking for your hand

(*it being sown over with Parma violets ......*)